Esau
Sullivan
Wesley
Nischal
Justice
Sabin
Cliff

Mossy Glenn Ranch
Chaps and Hope
Ropes and Dreams

Yes, Forever
Yes, Forever: Part One
Yes, Forever: Part Two
Yes, Forever: Part Three
Yes, Forever: Part Four
Yes, Forever: Part Five

Breaking the Devil

Totally Bound Publishing books by Bailey Bradford:

Southwestern Shifters

Rescued
Relentless
Reckless
Rendered
Resilience
Reverence
Revolution
Revenge

Southern Spirits

A Subtle Breeze
When the Dead Speak
All of the Voices
Wait Until Dawn
Aftermath
What Remains
Ascension
Whirlwind

Love in Xxchange

Rory's Last Chance
Miles to Go
Bend
What Matters Most
Ex's and O's
A Bit of Me
A Bit of You
In My Arms Tonight
Where There's A Will

Leopard's Spots

Levi
Oscar
Timothy
Isaiah
Gilbert

Mossy Glenn Ranch

SADDLES AND MEMORIES

BAILEY BRADFORD

Saddles and Memories
ISBN # 978-1-78184-689-6
©Copyright Bailey Bradford 2013
Cover Art by Posh Gosh ©Copyright 2013
Interior text design by Claire Siemaszkiewicz
Totally Bound Publishing

Published in 2014 by Totally Bound Publishing, Newland House, The Point, Weaver Road, Lincoln, LN6 3QN, United Kingdom.

Totally Bound Publishing is an imprint of Total-E-Ntwined Limited.

SADDLES AND MEMORIES

Dedication

Sometimes you need to step back and realise there are so many wonderful people around you, offering support.
To my patient and amazing editor, Eleanor, who is always a pleasure to work with, and to everyone involved in getting this book ready for publication.
Thank you.

Chapter One

Jesus, it was hot. Saul 'Salt' Johnson couldn't remember a Montana summer ever being so hellacious. Sweat was running down his back, tickling its way past the waistband of his jeans and making him want to scratch indecently. His brow was soaked, above and below the brim of his straw hat. Salt's eyes stung as much from the sweat dripping in them as from the God-awful bright sun.

There wasn't a cloud in sight in that bright blue sky, either. Salt could see the ranch land for miles, and past that, in the distance off to the south, the ridges and peaks of the Absaroka Mountains. He'd seen them once, up close-like, and had been awed by the majestic beauty of the mountains.

It'd made him feel tiny and inconsequential at the same time, driving home the fact that he wasn't anything important in the grand scheme of things. He'd live and die, and his body would rot, his bones turn to dust, but those mountains would still be there, reaching up into the sky.

Salt didn't take it personal, though. Man wasn't meant to be more enduring than those mountains. All a person had to do to see that was turn on the TV news or look at it online. Always fighting and killing, suppressing and hating. Salt didn't get it, but he reckoned he wasn't supposed to. Besides, he'd never been a particularly deep thinker.

The heat surely wasn't helping that any, either. Salt was thinking his brain might just be baking in his skull. He lifted his hat off, took his bandana from his neck, and wiped his face from hairline to chin.

The east pasture was showing signs of drought, never a good thing on a ranch, especially one just starting out. He'd heard the Mossy Glenn had been something to brag about years back. The last owner had run it into the ground, and maybe not many people could see beyond that, but Salt could easily envision the way the place must have looked before. New buildings with fresh paint, a good, strong fence line, grass so green it made you yearn to take a nap on it and fresh water flowing in the stream that cut across the land.

That water was still there, but flowing was a generous description of it. Trickled, that was what it did, but at least they had something in the stream. There were others not so lucky.

Salt quit woolgathering and got to his task. The stock tank was too low to put any more horses in the pasture. There wasn't much left of the pond, and the mud could be dangerous on a horse's ankles for starters. That was why Salt had moved the small herd of Quarter horses earlier. Now he was trying to judge whether it'd be better to have the stock tank filled, or start having someone look for a source of underground water. It just might be easier to do that and get some pipes running to a water trough. Give the horses a fresh source of water.

Of course, that depended on finding a water source. The stream wasn't an option, but there might be an underground well somewhere close enough to be serviceable.

Salt scratched his cheek, thinking of a dowser he'd seen about ten years back. The woman had used two y-shaped sticks to find a well on a ranch he'd been working back then. There'd been shit-talking by the cowhands, first because she was a she, and second because of the branches and the gossiping about dowsing being witchcraft.

But that lady had found water sure enough, and not one person dared to mutter under his breath around her after that. He wondered if Carlos would be open to having a dowser, preferably that same one, come walk his land.

Might take some time, Salt reasoned, so they were likely going to have to have the stock tank filled. It'd be costly. Everyone raised their prices in a drought, but the horses had to have water.

Filling the stock tank would help the grass stay green, too, or at least more of it than not. Salt gave a nod, decision made. They'd keep the tank filled, but if the ranch could afford it, it wouldn't hurt to check for another water source or two.

He heard the sound of an approaching vehicle and figured it'd be Rocky. She'd quickly become his best friend, much to Salt's surprise. While he was easy-going around other people, friendly and all that, he'd never really had close friends.

When he'd worked other ranches, he'd had to worry too much about hiding the fact that he was gay to let anyone close. A lifetime of keeping a distance between him and anyone else should have held up under Rocky's attempts at friendship, but they hadn't. Maybe he was just getting old.

Okay, at forty-five, he wasn't exactly ancient but he'd sure have thought he'd be more set in his ways. Then again, Rocky was a force to be reckoned with. Lord knew there wasn't anyone on the Mossy Glenn who'd snicker over her being a woman and live to talk about it. Cowboys could be some of the biggest misogynists, Salt could admit that. Didn't make them all evil, just ignorant in some places.

He turned and watched the battered white Ford F-250 coming down the road. Rocky waved to him and he flapped a hand in return. Then he checked the two-way radio on his hip. Volume was up and it was working, which meant Rocky hadn't tried reaching him on it and failed. He had driven the other truck out, too, so he didn't need a ride. That pretty much meant Rocky was coming out to chat, a rare but not totally unheard of thing for her to do.

Salt took the time to wipe his face down again while Rocky pulled up beside his truck. He strolled over as she was getting out. "What you doing out here, woman? You get lost again?"

Rocky flipped him off as she guffawed. "Aw, fuck you, Salt. I figured as long as you been out here, I'd better make sure you weren't buzzard food."

Salt was about to point out that there weren't any buzzards when he glanced up and saw that there were three of the birds circling way up in the air. "Huh. Guess they're waiting for me to vacate so they can drink. That or the smell of the stock tank is tricking them into thinking something died." Lord knew the mud reeked.

"Probably the last one," Rocky said as she ambled over. "They coulda drank from the stream."

"Yeah," Salt agreed. "So what are you doing out here?"

Rocky sighed and that wasn't like her at all. Salt looked at her, really examining her scrunched-up blue eyes, short, upturned nose and full mouth. Looking at it all together, he could see she wasn't happy at all. "What happened, Rock?" He wouldn't ask if she needed him to kick someone's ass because she could and would do that herself, but if she needed to talk, he could listen.

Rocky took her hat off with one hand and used the other to run her fingers through her short brown hair. She set the hat back on her head and exhaled like it was hurting her to do so. "Shelly dumped me."

Salt grimaced. He wasn't sure what to say to that. It wasn't like he'd had any relationships that were about anything more than getting off quick and not getting caught. Still, Rocky was his friend and all. Before he could figure out what to say, she started talking again.

"The thing is, I think maybe I loved the idea of her more than her, you know?" Rocky said, shoving her hands in her front jeans pockets. "Instant family, with her having kids and all. I really wanted kids."

"Don't see why you can't have any," Salt said, confused over that. "I mean, you could get artificially inseminated—"

Rocky's sharp burst of laughter cut him off. "Oh no, man, you don't get it. Just 'cause I have a uterus doesn't mean I'm the pregnant type anymore than you are, and the whole baby part of it..." She shook her head. "I like them from about four on up. The complete helplessness of a baby scares the ever-lovin' shit out of me. I'd even take a teenager over a baby."

Salt didn't have a preference one way or the other. He wasn't the father type, or the mother type. He loved his job too much, and he could admit he was too selfish to have kids. It was too bad other people weren't so honest. It'd spare a lot of kids some horrible — and deadly — abuse. Not that he'd ever hurt a kid if he did somehow magically end up with one, but he'd mess it up somehow. He just didn't think he'd be a good parent, period.

"And I thought I had the family I've always wanted, but I should have known better," Rocky was saying. "Shelly hasn't been returning my calls unless it's right before payday, and I bet that wasn't her sister who answered her phone last Saturday night when I called to see why Shelly didn't come out here like she was supposed to. I let that bitch walk all over me, didn't I?"

"You were sending her money?" Salt asked. "Didn't you two start dating right before you started here?"

Rocky glared at him. "Yeah, yeah, I'm a fuckin' idiot, I get it."

"No, you aren't." Boy, Salt could sure dig himself in deep. He put a hand on Rocky's shoulder. "You're just wanting someone who's as good and honest as you are, and people will take advantage of that." *There, that sounded pretty good.*

"Which translates into, I'm a desperate fuckin' idiot," Rocky snapped. "It's a damn good thing I count you as a friend, otherwise I'd think you were trying to insult me on purpose."

"I wasn't trying to insult you anyhow, purpose or accident," Salt said as he raised his hands up in front of himself. "I just don't rightly know what to say. She's a stupid bitch for using you, though." He rolled his lips in between his teeth and pressed down to keep from blurting out anything else insulting. Bad-mouthing Shelly was probably a huge mistake.

But Rocky cackled and slapped him on the shoulder. "There, see? That's how you comfort a friend who's been cheated on and dumped!"

Salt quit trying to keep quiet, letting his lips out from between his teeth. "Well, hell, Rock, I can bash your ex with you, no problem, but what happens if you two get back together?"

"We won't," Rocky assured him, wrinkling her nose at Salt. "Ugh. I've never ever taken a cheater back. And I might be an idiot, but I'm only a woman's idiot once. I bet Shelly is gonna be calling me come payday and trying to tell me she won't ever cheat again—huh."

That sounded like a thoughtful 'huh' to him, one he was intended to inquire about, so he did. "Huh what?"

Rocky scratched her chin. "You know, I just realised every girlfriend I've had has cheated on me. Maybe something's wrong with me."

"Other than having bad taste in women, I don't think so," Salt quickly informed her. "You might want to figure out why you keep picking the same kind of girlfriend. Seems to me I read something a while back about how people always gravitate to the familiar, even if it isn't any good for them. It's what we know, so it's safe even though it's going to hurt us."

If those words struck a little close to home for Salt, no one but him ever needed to know it.

"Yeah." Rocky pushed her hat back and looked up at the sky. "I need to do some of that introspection Oprah and Dr Phil used to yammer about on their TV shows."

"I never watched either of 'em," Salt admitted as they reached their trucks. "Good Lord, my back aches today. Think my mattress is older than I am." He arched and tried to keep from grimacing as his lower back muscles spasmed. "Damn."

Rocky spun him around and pushed him—not too gently, either—against the side of his truck. "I used to be a massage therapist ages ago," she told him right before she began pressing firmly against his lower back.

Salt forgot about his initial instinct to protest. He moaned pitifully, closed his eyes and all but melted against the truck while Rocky worked the cramps right out of his back. There were obviously benefits to having a best friend. Salt couldn't give a back rub comparable to the one he was getting, but he could do other things for Rocky, like listen to her talk and help her get over Shelly.

"Feel better?" she asked sometime later. Salt didn't know how long he'd been holding the truck in place while Rocky gave him the best massage he'd ever had.

"Kind of feel like Jell-O," he admitted as he opened his eyes. "Damn, Rocky. I'm feeling all kinds of loose."

Rocky slapped his butt. "Yeah, I bet you are. A good massage can do that to ya. And now that I have you all relaxed and grateful, you can go with me to the feed store."

Salt groaned and flopped around to press his back against the truck. He gave his friend a mock-glare. "I shoulda known there was a catch to that bit of bliss."

Rocky guffawed and patted his hand. "Aw, now, no whining. Carlos already said we both could go in and have lunch out. I thought it'd be nice, then we can go to the feed store and pick up the small order Troy called in."

"Yeah, okay." Salt hated going into town—he was a ranch hermit all the way—but he did what he had to. And eating away from Drake, the ranch chef he'd had a crush on, would probably be better for his digestion. Salt got embarrassed every time he thought about how he'd ever hoped for a chance with someone as sexy and sweet as Drake. He really should have known better.

"I need to wash up first. Meet me back at the bunk house?" Salt got a nod from Rocky. It looked like he had a lunch date with his best bud, then.

Chapter Two

Lunch at the diner had been good, but Salt couldn't help but compare the food to Drake's cooking, and frankly the food at the diner fell short of Drake's. That wasn't him mooning over Drake, either. Salt didn't think about Drake that way anymore, he was just embarrassed that he ever had in the first place. And the man was a damn good cook.

Why in the world Salt had been thinking about trying to have something serious with someone, with Drake, was a subject he'd been pondering on those nights when he couldn't sleep. He guessed it came down to finally being able to be out—not something he'd have been able to do and keep his job on any other of the ranches he'd worked on.

Because he'd loved being a cowboy, a ranch hand, more than he'd ever been interested in being in a steady relationship, Salt had kept himself closeted, only peeking out of that darkness when he knew it was safe and he could get off without getting busted. He'd thought love wasn't on the cards for him, wasn't sure it was possible, period. Then he'd got hired on at the Mossy Glenn. There was no way he could miss the love and devotion between Carlos, Troy and Will.

Seemed to Salt that if that kind of enduring love was possible for three men, it sure as shit should be possible for two. And, he was getting older. He didn't want to be alone for the rest of his life.

"Got your head in the clouds today." Rocky's voice pulled him right back to Earth.

"Yeah, guess so." Salt took a sip of his iced tea. "Was the pecan pie good?" Rocky had got a piece, but Salt had passed. Dessert wasn't a big deal to him.

Rocky licked her lips, her blue eyes gleaming. "Oh, hell yeah, that was the best pecan pie I've had in ages. Bet even Drake couldn't make a better one."

"Probably not," Salt agreed easily. He honestly didn't care one way or the other.

"Would you like a refill?"

Salt glanced up at the waitress. Her nametag declared her to be Jen. She looked to be younger than Salt, and someone Rocky kept sneaking appreciative peeks at when good ol' Jen wasn't looking.

"No thanks," Salt told her. The woman was attractive, he reckoned, not that he was the best judge. "We'll just take the bill."

"The pie was awesome," Rocky gushed effusively. "I'm gonna be coming back for more, soon. Pie, I mean. Pecan pie. Because it's so good." Rocky's cheeks went ruddy and Salt could see the trepidation building in her eyes.

"She really likes the pie," Salt joked, hoping to ease Rocky's discomfort. Jen just looked torn between amusement and confusion. *Poor Rocky, she's crushing on a straight woman.* That wasn't going to end well, although maybe it'd peter out and Rocky would find someone to reciprocate her interest.

"It is good pie," Jen said in a soft voice. "It's my grandma's recipe."

"You made it?" Rocky asked, and damn, but she sounded a little too smarmy there whether she meant to or not.

Jen's cheeks turned pink and she darted a nervous look to Salt before turning it back on Rocky. "Er, yes. I—let me get your ticket."

"I'm such an idiot," Rocky whispered as Jen hurried off. Rocky hissed and covered her face with her hands. "Oh, God, next time shut me up."

Salt nudged her knee with his under the table. "It wasn't that bad. I just think you're lusting up the wrong tree."

Rocky peeked out at him from between her fingers. "Lusting up the wrong tree? Stop mixing metaphors or whatever that's called. You're gonna give me a run for the money in the ridiculous department."

Salt shrugged. "I'm not trying to impress anybody, so I don't really care what they think."

The diner door swung open and a tall, stocky young man in overalls came in, battered ball cap on and a big, goofy grin in place. "Hey, Ma, did you save me some meatloaf?"

Salt thought the kid looked familiar and it took him a second to place him. Barney something or another, who'd come out and helped paint over the graffiti on the barns a while back.

Just about the same time he figured that out, Barney picked Jen up in a hug that made her squeak. "Put me down, son!"

Barney grinned and gave Jen a twirl. "Aw, Mom, you know I gotta sweep you off your feet before that guy you went out with last week runs off with you."

Jen smacked Barney's shoulder. "Craig and I aren't running off anywhere."

Rocky sighed and Salt gave her his attention. "Yeah, wrong tree and all that. Here's my share of the bill plus the tip. I'll meet you outside."

A few minutes later, Salt joined Rocky on the sidewalk. The sun was just as bright, the heat just as brutal, as it had been earlier. Maybe even more so. "Let's get the damn feed and go. At least we'll have the AC in the truck for a while before we have to get all sweaty again."

"Sounds like a plan." Rocky gave the diner one last glance. Salt nudged her arm. "Yeah, yeah. She just seemed like the opposite of the type of chick I usually pick." Rocky guffawed. "Well, and ain't she? She's straight, they weren't."

Salt thought silence on the subject was the best option he had. They strolled to the truck. "You driving?"

"Nah, you can." Rocky tossed him the keys. "I want to sit back and relax once we have the feed loaded."

At the feed store, Salt noticed an unfamiliar truck in the lot. The truck was a shiny red Dodge 2500, and it had advertisements all over it for a feed company he'd never heard of in his thirty-plus years of ranching. He saw the words 'organic' and 'non-GMO' along with lines about absolutely nothing added that included chemicals and antibiotics and such.

Pretty much the way it used to be, he figured. Salt parked up front by the doorway.

"Health food for cows and horses, sheep and goats," Rocky muttered. "Gonna have 'em doing yoga next thing you know."

Salt chuckled even though he thought that fewer chemicals and additives in feed—for any animal, human or otherwise—was probably a good thing. More and more, he was becoming aware of what he was putting in his mouth, thanks to news reports and Internet stories.

Probably, like wanting a long-term relationship, it had to do with him getting older. Salt liked living, and he intended to go on doing it as long as possible.

"Bet I'd be richer than George Strait in no time at all," Rocky continued as they walked inside the feed store. "Probably just have the cows and other critters standing like they always do and call it something like Animal Reaches Earth and Sun pose, ya know?"

Salt opened his mouth up to answer but was struck mute by the sight of a man across the store. Rocky didn't seem to notice, she just kept chattering along, but Salt couldn't look away from eyes so dark they might have been black. Salt blinked, then he took in the whole picture the man made.

He was wearing a white felt hat, a blue and white checked pearl-snap western shirt. Add in Wranglers so worn and tight that Salt could tell he was blessed with a nice package, and the man was sexy in that worn cowboy-looking way that always turned Salt's crank.

The twitch of his dick snapped Salt out of his rude ogling. Granted, the other guy'd been looking right back at him, but still. They were out in public, in a small and not close to tolerant place. Salt dragged his gaze away and settled it on Rocky, who was still rambling on about sheep poses.

Salt herded her towards the customer service desk. "Hey there, Teddy," he said, greeting the sales clerk. He was glad Teddy was working. Teddy was always friendly, and he wasn't hard on the eyes, either, with his red hair sprinkled with white at the temples.

"Hey, Salt, Rocky. What you going on about?" Teddy asked, cocking his head at Rocky.

Rocky proceeded to tell Teddy about her idea and the inspiration for it, mentioning the red Dodge outside.

A tingle of awareness shot through Salt. In fact, it felt like his entire back was warming up, as if he could feel the heat of a stare. Despite Rocky's continuing rambling, Salt heard the click of boot heels on the floor. Why didn't Rocky or Teddy seem to be aware of the electric current in the air?

Salt tensed, then he had to turn, at least enough to peer behind him. Sure enough, the handsome stranger was approaching. Those dark eyes met his gaze and Salt felt a sexual thrill that made his dick do more than twitch. He turned back around, silently scolding himself and telling his pecker to mind its manners.

"Hey, Andy," Teddy called out, when Rocky paused. "This here young lady has been plumb inspired by your feed."

Rocky went red as a stop sign. Salt had known she was joking, but Teddy...wasn't always the brightest star in the sky, even though he was nice.

"Rocky here's talking about starting some kind of animal yoga 'cause of all the health nuts—" Teddy glanced at her. "That's what you called 'em, right?"

Rocky made a strangled sound and closed her eyes.

"I imagine Rocky was joking around, Teddy," Andy said in a deep, rich voice that reminded Salt of dark chocolate and sin. "I'd be happy to explain the benefits of using my feed instead of any of the bigger names' merchandise."

The man was gracious. He could have made Rocky feel like a fool, or laid on the guilt instead of being a decent human being. Rocky stopped trying to hide behind her closed lids, opening her eyes and sighing. She turned and Salt did too.

Jesus. Salt had to bite his tongue to keep from saying it out loud, but hell, standing face to face with Andy was like being slugged in the gut with desire so intense Salt just wanted to fold over and moan out his need. Andy's eyes were every bit as dark as the best chocolate, and his lips, that thinner top one especially, just called for sucking on.

"I'm glad you're not the thin-skinned type," Rocky said, offering Andy her hand to shake. "Seems like no one has a sense of humour no more."

Andy smiled, and the change in expression turned him from simply attractive to devastatingly handsome. Salt was close to swooning, something he'd always thought only old uptight people did. He didn't know why this one man was so appealing to him, didn't know what stars were in perfect alignment or where his horoscope was meeting up with which planet, but goddamn, he wanted Andy, wanted him bad.

"I know what you mean," Andy said. "We're so politically correct you can't crack a joke."

"Yeah, exactly." Rocky tucked her hands in her back pockets. "I reckon we could talk to our boss about you coming out and explaining this feed of yours. I don't see what's wrong with what we use, but I know I'm not ever gonna understand all the scientific parts of whatever it is you'll be saying. What do you think, Salt?" She looked at him.

Salt nodded. "Yeah, we can talk to Carlos, see if he's interested." *Oh thank God my voice didn't crack.* As dry as his mouth had gone when he turned to face Andy, Salt was surprised he could even speak. "I tell you what, you got a card?"

"I do." Andy took one out of his shirt pocket. "I'm Andy Calder, co-owner of Organic Feeds."

"Saul Johnson, just a ranch hand at the Mossy Glenn." Salt took the card, then as soon as he tucked it into his pocket, Andy held his hand out to shake. "People call me Salt." Oh, but he almost whimpered when Andy's warm hand clasped his. Salt had decades of calluses built up on his hands. They weren't anywhere near to being the most sensitive part of his body, but right then, as they shook, he'd have bet every nerve in his body had transported to his right hand.

"Salt." Andy gave him a half-grin and licked his lips. "My favourite spice."

Salt felt his eyes widen at the brazen flirt. Rocky chortled and started chattering at Teddy about the feed order.

Andy didn't release Salt's hand. In fact, he used it to tug Salt a half a step closer. "I've heard a lot of things about the Mossy Glenn," Andy said in a rough whisper. "You should give me a call when you're done working today and give me a private tour of the place."

"Wouldn't be much privacy from the second you got there," Salt managed to get out. "Cowboys are a nosy bunch. We'd be spied on unless we rode pretty far out, and if you're wanting to sell feed to my employers, I don't know that that'd be the first impression you'd want to make with them."

Andy stroked his palm and released his hand. "Maybe not the best idea, then, but you... I don't beat around the bush, Salt. I'd love to feel your mouth on me."

Salt was old enough not to be shy, but he hadn't had the freedom to be out and proud until only recently.

He didn't know what to say, how to handle such a come-on out in a public place that wasn't a skeezy gay bar.

But he did know that he wanted the same thing Andy did. That gave him the impetus to keep from freaking out. "You got a room in town?"

Andy shook his head. "No, but I will have. Won't hurt to stay in town a couple of days and see if your bosses will let me talk to them while I'm here."

Salt's entire body heated with excitement. He was going to get laid, by Andy, who was the best-looking man he'd ever been granted the chance to hook up with. "There's the Super 8 Motel, unless you want to drive about half an hour for something fancier."

"Super 8 will do just fine." Andy brushed his knuckles over Salt's thickening dick. "I'll be ordering some pizza and popping open a beer about six. You have a phone so I can text you my room number?"

"I do." Salt waited until Andy had his fancy phone out, then he gave Andy his number.

"You have mine on the card," Andy said as he tucked his phone away. "I'll see you this evening. Be ready for me."

Salt almost lost the battle to keep from getting a full-blown hard-on at that point. He nodded and forced himself to turn around, get back to business. Even so, as he joined in the conversation with Rocky and Teddy, his mind was on the coming evening.

It had been over a year since he'd been with anyone. Even then, most of the hookups he'd had were just quickies. There'd been the occasional night spent with someone, the freedom to touch and discover what one another liked, but it had been damned rare. Rare enough he couldn't even remember the last guy he'd been with that way.

He couldn't sleep over at the motel, but he could stay until they were both well and truly sated.

Salt was very aware of Andy's presence in the feed store, of the clomp of his footsteps. He could see Andy in his peripheral vision, doing something on his phone over by the bags of food.

Salt's phone vibrated. "Excuse me," he said to Teddy and Rocky as he took the phone from his belt clip. Salt opened his phone and saw the text message from Andy.

Well, he guessed he knew what Andy had been doing on his phone. His text had the room number at the Super 8, along with the repeated order that Salt be ready for him.

Salt hadn't been so turned on since he'd first lost his virginity. Maybe not even then. He was going to be ready all right. He texted Andy back, because there was something the man needed to know.

You'd better be ready too.

Chapter Three

Salt took some ribbing from Rocky, who hadn't been as oblivious to him and Andy flirting as she'd seemed. Of course the other ranch hands picked up on it and by the time Salt was on his way to the Super 8, even Carlos, Troy and Will had teased him.

He didn't mind—he liked the camaraderie at the Mossy G. Besides, he was squeaky clean inside and out. Andy was waiting on him, and he was going to have a damned good time, barring Andy just being a shitty lover. Salt didn't think that'd be the case. Andy was too confident to be bad in bed.

The drive to Ashville seemed to take twice as long, and by the time Salt pulled up in front of room 113, his dick was already half-hard from all the things he'd imagined him and Andy doing. He parked the truck and shut it off. Salt did a quick check of himself in the rearview, then he tugged his hat down just a hair in front.

Salt didn't lie to himself about his appearance. He was forty-five and had spent more time outside than inside. The sun had darkened his face, left deep proof of his lack of sunscreen use etched into it. His black hair was going to be more white than not soon.

But he was still trim, tall and lean with tightly honed muscles. Granted, parts of him were so white they might blind a person, but none of him was bad to look at. Though he wouldn't win any beauty contests, either.

Salt unbuckled and got out of the truck. He shut the door then strode over to Andy's room. Before he got to it, Andy was standing in the doorway wearing obscenely low-hanging sweats that showed off an inch or two of his pubes above the waistband. He didn't have a shirt on, so his tanned torso was on display. Andy had broad shoulders and a nice amount of brown chest hair. He didn't have a chiselled six-pack, but he wasn't overweight, either. He was solid, and damn, he looked good.

"Come on in, cowboy," Andy rumbled as he stepped back. Salt could see that his cock was already beginning to rise, and there was no mistaking it for anything other than huge. It made Salt clench his ass in anticipation of feeling it spreading him open.

Salt didn't get more than clear of the door than Andy slammed it shut. Andy grabbed him by the shoulders, and Salt thought it was going to be hard and fast, Andy overpowering him or trying to—but no. Andy held him still and just stared at him, maybe studying his features, though for what, Salt didn't know.

It should have made him nervous, being inspected like a bull up for auction, but it didn't. There was a warmth in Andy's expression that made it clear he was enjoying the view. That, and Andy kneaded Salt's shoulders instead of just keeping his hands still.

Andy flicked his glance down to Salt's lips. "Do you kiss?"

Salt hadn't often, but only because of the nature of the men he'd been with. Neither he nor them had been interested in anything above the belt. "Yeah." There was no question that they both wanted it.

Andy tugged him closer. They pressed together from knee to chest, Andy's cock a hot brand against Salt's. They were evenly matched in height, which was nice. Andy ran his hands up the sides of Salt's neck and Salt settled on a loose grip of Andy's bare hips. Those sweats had to be hanging up on Andy's dick.

Andy took Salt's cowboy hat off and gave it a sailing toss onto the small table. Without anything else in the way, he cupped the back of Salt's neck. Salt tipped his head to the left and moved it forward just as Andy did.

The instant their lips touched, Salt moaned and closed his eyes. He clenched his hands, squeezing Andy's hips as Andy suckled on his bottom lip. Andy brought his other hand around to frame Salt's jaw. Salt inhaled through his nose as he opened his mouth wider, hoping to encourage Andy to bring his tongue on in.

Andy licked Salt's lips, tracing the line of them then wetting them each, nibbling on them until Salt was on the verge of begging for that kiss. Then Andy slid his tongue in and laid claim to every inch of Salt's mouth. All Salt could do was hang on and try to keep up. He surely wasn't going to gain control of the kiss. Andy clearly had more experience in this area, and Salt was fine with it.

He met Andy's thrust of tongue with greedy sucks and barely muffled whimpers. Andy's flesh was so warm and taut under Salt's hands, Salt didn't think he'd ever tire of touching him.

It didn't matter that they were standing in a cheap motel room, that they didn't know each other — Salt had been in that position more times than he could count. All that did matter was the need welling inside Salt, seeping out of his pores and bleeding onto Andy.

Andy growled into the kiss and his grip firmed up until it was almost painful. Almost, but not quite. Salt jerked on Andy's hips, needing so bad he wasn't sure he wouldn't come in his pants. His cock was pinned painfully behind the denim, and he wanted to be naked, or at least get his cock free, now before it got damaged.

He got a hand between them and began working his belt buckle open. Why'd he dress in his finest? It wasn't as if he'd thought his clothes were going to stay on for long, and the belt he had on was trickier to unbuckle than the one he usually wore.

Frustration had him nipping at Andy's tongue. Andy cursed, grinned and gave Salt the force he'd been expecting at first. He was driven back, stumbling as Andy just barrelled forward. The back of his legs hit the bed at the same time Andy gave him a push, and Salt toppled happily right on over.

Andy shoved his sweats down with one hand while keeping Salt pinned at the belly with the other. Salt was still trying to get his buckle undone. When he saw Andy's big, thick cock spring free of those sweats, Salt froze for a second, then he moaned and tried to reach for that monster.

"Ah-ah," Andy said in an almost musical way. "You get that belt off so we can suck each other. Then we can eat, have a beer or two and get ready for round two. This time isn't going to take either of us long, I'm thinking."

"Not on my end, it won't," Salt agreed. He went back to getting his belt and pants undone. Andy let go of his stomach and straddled one of Salt's calves backwards. "Jesus, Andy! How'm I supposed to fucking think with that ass pointing my way?" And it was a very fine ass, plump and smooth, not a hair on it anywhere to be seen.

Andy looked over his shoulder and leered. "It's not like you can fuck this ass as long as your dick's stuck behind that denim."

"You have a point," Salt mumbled. He got the buckle open and Andy grabbed Salt's boot and began tugging it off.

By the time Salt was shimmying his pants down, Andy had Salt's boots and socks off. "On your side, man," Andy told him.

Andy crawled onto the bed and kissed him again, kissed him until Salt was breathless, then Andy turned and flopped down so that his face was right at Salt's groin.

And without further hesitation, Andy grabbed Salt by the base of his cock, used his other hand to cup Salt's balls, then he sucked the crown of Salt's shaft into the warm, wet perfection of his mouth. Salt grunted and tried not to let his eyes cross as he palmed Andy's cock in return.

It had enough girth that Salt's thumb and forefinger didn't quite meet at the base. Thick veins lined it, making it what some guys might think of as an ugly cock, but Salt loved the way they made Andy's pecker look strong, powerful.

He licked up the length of it, then nuzzled Andy's balls while Andy sank his hot mouth farther down on

Salt's dick. He rolled Salt's balls, gave them a perfect tug and Salt had to close his eyes and focus on the blow job he was trying to give as he hitched his top leg up to give Andy more room to play.

Andy's fat shaft made Salt's jaws ache. Of course, he was out of practice, too. The last few encounters he'd had were hand jobs. But the way Andy's dick filled his mouth was wonderful, like a sensual invasion spreading from inside him to the outside.

Salt thumbed one of the thick veins as he worked more of Andy's length into his mouth. He used his tongue to trace the underside of Andy's cap, then to follow one vein in particular. He wouldn't be able to take all of Andy's cock into his mouth and throat, but he wouldn't need to. Andy would still breach Salt's throat with Salt's hand ringing Andy's base.

The salty tang of pre-cum hit his tongue and Salt moaned around his mouthful. At the same time, Andy moved a finger back and began rubbing Salt's sweet spot between his nuts and hole. Salt's heart stuttered and he clenched his ass before beginning to thrust, giving in to the need that was consuming him. He tried to keep a tight seal on Andy's cock, but his orgasm blindsided him, slamming into Salt so quickly and forcefully that he jerked his head back and shouted in surprise.

He tried to curl in on himself as bliss swept over him, but Andy was there, his wet cock tapping Salt's chin.

* * * *

The man was a stone-cold stud, and Andy had wanted him from the second he'd walked into the feed store. Andy loved men—young, old, skinny, chubby, heavier than that, he didn't care, as long as they were legal and he was attracted to them. So it wasn't a surprise to find himself nearly drooling over a man who was probably at least five or six years older than him. It was hard to tell with sun-weathered cowboys.

But Salt had that whipcord lean look to him, and a hungry, lustful gleam in his eye. He had a tiny, tight ass, and nipples so small and dark Andy would have a month's worth of jerk-off material just thinking about how he could bruise those tits up.

Andy hadn't seen them of course, not when Salt first came into the feed store. All he'd seen was that lived-in look, the confidence and those beautiful light brown eyes. Fuck, but Salt had gorgeous eyes, large and tilted down just slightly at the corners, making him look sleepy, sexy, utterly fuckable.

And now Andy had the man in his bed, had the taste of his cum in his mouth, and he wasn't anywhere near satisfied. Salt had come apart for him like perfection, unwrapped a layer at a time at first, then Salt had jolted, his cock spurting his load.

Andy rolled Salt onto his back. If Andy didn't come soon, he was going to scream. He reached down and pushed at his cock. Salt wasn't slow at all, not now that his climax had eased off. He opened his mouth up and sucked Andy, hard.

Andy went tight from his thighs to his belly, trying not to thrust. His dick was a problem for some guys, at least when it came to giving head. None of them had ever taken him in all the way, and that was okay. Swallowing his whole dick wasn't a requirement for Andy to think a blow job was mind-meltingly good.

Salt added even more suction, and Andy gasped. His balls were pushed, pulled, keeping him right at the edge of pleasure and pain. Then Salt began really bobbing his head, flicking his tongue, and Andy had to thrust, at least a little. Salt's hand at the base of his dick would keep Andy from choking the man. He grabbed onto Salt's thighs and let himself go, fucking Salt's mouth like he had an open invitation to do so. He guessed he did since Salt was making happy groaning sounds, and he wasn't shoving Andy off him.

When Salt tongued his slit, Andy froze. Salt did it again, then he pulled off and pushed at it with a fingertip. Andy's head swam, a sound filling it like a hive of bees had settled in his skull.

Salt sucked Andy's balls into his mouth, and pressed on his slit again while jacking his cock. Andy keened and rutted as cum pulsed from his shaft.

Salt murmured words Andy couldn't understand. He was lost in his release and when he started to come down from it, Salt began licking his cock. Andy almost skittered right off the bed, but Salt grabbed him by the hips and rolled them again. Then Salt proceeded to lick the cum off Andy's skin, starting at his quivering thighs.

Andy hadn't ever had a lover take so much care cleaning him. Usually it was a washcloth or a wet wipe, if it was any cleaning off at all. Most often, Andy headed to a shower and whoever he'd had sex with left. He hadn't had time to linger, and whoever he'd been with hadn't been interested in doing so.

Yet he wanted that pizza and beer with Salt, and he wanted another round or two with the man. God, but he wanted to see Salt gasping and wriggling as Andy pushed his fat dick into Salt's ass. Just the idea of it had Andy's dick trying to wave howdy.

"You young ones," Salt mumbled before moving around to flop beside Andy. "You still want me to hang around?"

Andy snorted. "I can't be that much younger than you." He wasn't going to risk guessing wrong though. "Maybe two or three years. And yes, I do. Don't think you're leaving without giving me a ride, cowboy. I want to see how you look riding my dick."

Salt smiled just a little, and something weird happened in Andy's heart. He dismissed the fluttering warmth as heartburn. It'd been happening lately.

"I know you're being kind, smart guy like you," Salt said as he closed his eyes. "I know you're smart because you're co-owner of the feed company you're representing. I'm forty-five, Andy, and you can't be a day over thirty."

Huh. Andy had been off on his private estimation. "I'm actually thirty-seven." Then something occurred to him. "Hey, were you curbing your guess on my age to keep from offending me?"

Salt opened one eye. "Depends."

Andy frowned at him. "I thought you were only five years older than me, so you're older than you look." Then Andy propped himself up on his elbows. "I hope you're not coming back with a 'and so are you'."

Salt laughed and patted Andy's stomach. "Naw, you're a fine-looking man, Andy. Calm down."

"I am calm, just contemplating face cream." Andy chortled. Him and face cream weren't ever going to happen.

"All's I knew for sure was that you were younger, and so sexy you made my balls ache," Salt finally told him.

Andy decided he didn't need to worry about his age or wrinkles or anything else. He had only recently started noticing things like the occasional grey hair and the way his joints ached after a really hard workout.

"I need to get up and order the pizza," he said, sitting up. "What do you want on yours?"

Salt shrugged. "I'm not picky. Put it in front of me, and I'll eat it."

"Really," Andy dragged out, arching one eyebrow.

Salt grinned at him and blew him a kiss.

It was such a silly, playful thing, but Andy couldn't recall anything like it since maybe college, when there'd been one guy he'd dated for a few weeks. He'd just been busy for so long...

"I don't really get to do the hanging around afterwards thing," Salt said, and it so echoed the direction Andy's own thoughts were going in that Andy was startled. He thought he hid it well.

"Yeah? Me neither. Life's been busy, you know?" Andy hated how shallow that made him sound. There was more to it than that, but he didn't go spilling his guts to everyone. Anyone, really.

"Just wasn't possible for me." Salt wiggled like he was trying to get comfortable on the bed. "Being a gay cowboy? Yeah, they've made movies about that shit. Don't get a happy ending that way."

"But the Mossy Glenn hires family." Andy had heard that. It couldn't just be gossip.

"Yup, they sure do, and let me tell you, that's got its own hardships." Salt scooted and sat with his back against the headboard. "You have no idea how much teasing I took for going out to get laid tonight. Of course, most of them thought it was a date." Salt shook his head. "I work with a bunch of romantic fools."

Andy had to chuckle at the image he had of Salt being ribbed by his friends. "Ah well, I guess they just want you happy. You happy?"

"Very." Salt's stomach growled and he patted it. "Hungry, too."

Andy stood up and stretched, liking the way Salt's gaze went over him like a warm caress. "Yeah, pizza."

When the food arrived, they sat on the bed eating, drinking beer and watching crappy television shows. Somehow, Andy found himself enjoying the company, laughing with Salt, trading stories about their stupid youth tricks and bad hookups.

He couldn't figure out how it happened, but the last thing he remembered was leaning against Salt and thinking it'd been a good evening, one of the best he'd ever had.

Chapter Four

As much as he hated to, Salt settled for letting Andy sleep instead of waking him up for a goodbye. He wished that Andy had fucked him, but honestly, the night had been so relaxing, and the company so good, that Salt was more than satisfied with what had happened between them. It'd been unique for him, and he'd liked the companionship.

Reminded him of hanging with the guys and gals at the ranch, except he'd felt the embers of desire all the time he'd been there with Andy. Nothing pressing, just the attraction twanging between them.

Andy was sprawled out on the bed, snoring softly, his mouth open and looking like he just needed to be loved on. Salt didn't want to risk being late to work in the morning, and besides, Andy hadn't asked him to sleep over. Salt wasn't sure what the rules were in situations like the one he was in. Leaving seemed the wisest choice.

It also seemed kind of rude. Salt spotted the little notepad and pen on the table. At least they'd dozed off with the lamp on so he could see. It'd sure made getting dressed easier. He jotted down a quick note about not wanting to wake Andy, and needing to leave. Before he could stop himself, he added that he was hoping Andy still wanted to see him ride.

Salt left it at that. He put his hat on and left the room, hanging the Do Not Disturb sign up on the outside knob. The rumble of the truck engine shouldn't wake Andy up, Salt figured. There'd been plenty of coming and going from people and their vehicles all night. Salt got in his truck and started up. He buckled his seat belt and checked behind him before backing out.

It was a little after one in the morning when he pulled up to the bunkhouse. While everyone was sleeping, he had no hope of getting inside and to his room unheard. As nosy as the crew was, someone would be sleeping with one eye open, and sure enough, that one person was Rocky. She didn't even try to hide it, sitting up on the couch, snuffling and opening her eyes when he shut the front door.

"Don't start," he warned when she opened her mouth. "I'm tired, and want to get to bed. You can grill me after I get some sleep."

"'Kay," she agreed easily, getting up off the couch. "Now that I know you ain't dead in some skeezy motel room, I can get some real sleep too."

Salt was a little touched that she really seemed concerned for him. It was moments like those—when he was faced with the reality that some people really *did* care what happened to him for reasons other than needing him to work—that showed Salt he'd moved forward in life. Used to be he had to keep everyone at a distance, and that'd been fine, but now he was making friends. He liked it.

If he wanted a little more, well, he couldn't dwell on that. Salt was relieved that Rocky ambled right on into her room. He went into his and sighed as he stretched. He was a bit stiff in places he wasn't used to being stiff in. All in all, he was in great shape, but he wasn't as flexible as he used to be, and there were certain positions involved in sex that one didn't find themselves in at any other times.

Salt took off his hat and set it on the dresser. He unbuttoned his shirt and ran one hand over his chest. It sent tingles of arousal through him, especially when he imagined it being Andy's hand. He wondered if he'd ever hear from Andy again, and whether the man regretted not getting to fuck him.

Jesus, he was getting melancholy in his old age.

No, I'm fucking lonely.

That realisation eradicated any arousal he'd been feeling. He thought of Carlos, Will and Troy, so content and loving in their threesome, and of Drake and Ian, a newly minted couple who seemed well-suited as could be. Gay men could live happily ever after, if those men were anything to judge by. Salt hadn't really thought it possible before, at least not for a cowboy.

He wanted that for himself, wanted it badly as he stood almost naked in his room in the middle of the night, smelling Andy's scent on his skin. Maybe it was melancholy, maybe it was exhaustion, but Salt wished he'd been able to stay in that motel room and sleep with Andy. Wake up the next day and take time exploring each other. Shower together, laughing, teasing, touching. Breakfast together, chatting and planning their day or maybe even their week.

Salt shook himself and firmly locked down his little fantasies. He was being a ridiculous old fool.

But even so, he still dreamt of things he'd only just started believing in.

* * * *

Breakfast entailed a lot of ribbing from the crew, but Salt didn't really mind. Also, it kept Rocky from being able to grill him, though he had no illusions that she'd be held off for long. He hadn't stepped off the porch into the early morning sunlight before Rocky was at his side poking him in the ribs.

"Come on, dish. I want to know if I need to smack that sales boy before he shows up later."

Salt just about stumbled down the porch steps. "What? Why would he show up later?"

Rocky snorted and snickered as he flailed his arms trying to keep from plopping down on his butt as his boot heel slipped on the last step. "Because I gave Carlos his card, told him about what he was selling, and that you were off fucking the guy," Rocky informed him.

"What?" Salt squeaked spinning around to glare at her. He didn't ever want such an overshare of gossip going on. "You didn't tell him that last part!"

Rocky had a good, long laugh at him, one of those bend-at-the-waist-and-make-your-eyes-water kind of laughs. By the time she could gasp out a 'no', Salt was getting irritated. She took a few breaths and swiped at her eyes. "Chill out, Salt. I wouldn't tell him about the fucking part, that's your business. It's not like everyone here doesn't know what you were off doing. Not a one of us thought you were playing dominoes with Andy. Sheesh. You can be such a prude." Rocky cackled at him then went on. "I did tell Carlos the rest, though, and he was actually interested. Said Will had been harping on him about organic this and non-GMO that, so he'd give your guy a call in the morning, see if he'd come out today."

"He's not my guy," Salt muttered, but he sure was feeling warm and fluttery on the inside. "We just hooked up for the night."

Rocky gave him a doubtful look. "Uh-huh. I think there was more than a one-night stand's worth of sexual tension between you two."

Salt didn't really have a reply for that, because, truth be told, he hadn't got enough of Andy.

"I'm going to go see to the pastures, take the newbies out and show them what's what. Why don't you—"

"I'm not hanging around here waiting to see if Andy shows up," Salt said, cutting Rocky off. Even if he did want to do just that, he wouldn't. "I got a job to do, Rocky. Mooning about like some lovesick fool for a guy I just got off with and don't really know? That's ridiculous." Plus, he'd probably come off as a stalker or something. "I'll take that one new guy, Ramsey, and have him check the horses in the North pasture with me. Who's in the barns?"

They worked out who would be where and doing what, then Salt found Ramsey and got on with doing his job. If he thought more often about Andy than he was comfortable with, well, he told himself it was just because it'd been so long since he'd been with anyone else. It had nothing to do with that longing he'd just acknowledged, or the way he kept seeing Andy's smile in his mind.

* * * *

Waking up alone wasn't unexpected, but for some reason, it sent Andy's mood plummeting. He'd known Salt had to get back to the ranch, but he guessed he'd been hoping maybe Salt would head back later.

It wasn't just because Andy had wanted to fuck him, either. That realisation was almost enough to send Andy running for home. He wasn't sure what was going on with him, but it was unusual.

Then he found the short note written by Salt. The man had surprisingly elegant handwriting, almost artistic, really. Andy carefully lifted the note from the rest of the pad. He carried it over to the bed and sat on the edge of the mattress while he read Salt's words.

There was nothing special about them, really, and yet hope and something very much like joy bubbled up inside Andy. He wanted to see this man again, talk to Salt, touch him. They'd had a good time. Andy knew it wasn't just him. Salt had laughed and they'd talked more than anything else. It'd been different, and Andy wanted more of it.

That didn't mean strings and a commitment. Salt probably didn't want either of those things any more than Andy did. Yet when he told himself that, Andy's gut went tight and that budding joy kind of just snuffled itself right out.

Andy groaned and rubbed his forehead with one hand, still holding the note with the other. What was wrong with him? It'd been a rough decade or so. Longer, even, but he'd thought he was okay. Living his life the way he wanted to now, finally.

Except he was beginning to suspect that wasn't the case.

His cell phone rang and his heart raced. Andy scooted up the bed until he could snatch his phone off the nightstand. He saw the local area code and his heart just about beat right out of his chest. There was something like hope burning in there.

"Hello?" he said after answering the call. He sounded a little breathless, but Andy put that down to moving so quick to grab the phone.

When he heard the drawling voice over the line, he knew instantly it wasn't Salt. His good mood shot downhill like a rollercoaster on that first steep drop. Good hell, he was going to have to get on some medication if his moods kept swinging all over the place.

But he listened and after a few minutes, he was back to feeling almost cheery again. He had an appointment at the Mossy Glenn in two hours to meet with the foreman and try to convince him to buy Organic Feeds' line of products. Carlos had sounded like a no-nonsense kind of man, so Andy firmly told himself not to bullshit him.

Some customers liked being fed a line, pandered to. They expected to be haggled with and for Andy to be kind of...smarmy. He hated playing the part, but experience had taught him to mould himself into whatever the customer wanted. The sale was all that mattered to the other company investors.

Lately, that kind of acting had begun to eat away at his conscience. He had moments where he doubted whether success was worth sacrificing his integrity. Oh, it wasn't that the product wasn't the best on the market—it was. Just sometimes he would like to be himself, and not put on a false front. There were days where potential customers were rude as hell, and Andy would have gladly told them where they could stick their business. He wouldn't, though, but he was beginning to think sales really wasn't his career calling.

In fact, he had a lot of moments where he asked himself why he bothered anymore. It wasn't like he had Destry or Ty depending on him now.

Andy stopped his thoughts from going any further in that direction. It would send him into a frame of mind that sure wasn't conducive for sales.

Besides, there was a chance of seeing Salt again, without having to break down and call the man. It'd been forever and a day since Andy had done anything like that. For years it'd just been 'wham bam' and 'see ya later'. It'd had to be. He wasn't sure he actually had the balls to call Salt, and was glad he might not have to.

Surely if we see each other, lust'll carry us past any awkward shit. He was fairly certain Salt was still into him, otherwise why even leave a note?

Andy's optimism kicked in and he whistled while got ready to head out. The note he tucked carefully into his wallet before he showered. Salt's scent still lingered on him, and he kind of hated to wash it off, which was silly and romantic and not like him at all. Andy scrubbed twice, hard enough to leave his skin red, as if punishing it for trying to hang onto Salt's aroma.

Good hell, he was a mess sometimes. Andy huffed and turned off the shower. He dried off with the towel he took down from the bar. The towel was thin and not soft at all like the ones he had back at his apartment in Helena. Not very big, either. Andy dropped the towel on the side of the tub then went about making himself presentable.

He'd managed to kill a half hour by the time he was dressed. Andy packed up his few items and left the motel room. He debated checking out, then decided to go ahead and do so. If there was any reason for him to stay another night, he'd just book a room again. It wasn't like the motel was crowded.

Breakfast consisted of McDonald's coffee and the healthy breakfast bars he'd brought with him. Last night he'd splurged with pizza and beer. Usually he was more particular—God knew he loved pizza and beer, though. Sometimes a man just had to indulge.

Eating while driving wasn't Andy's favourite thing to do either. He parked at the side of McDonald's. As much as he wanted to head to the ranch, he made himself wait until he'd finished his food. Andy wadded up the trash and stuffed it into a small container he kept in the truck for garbage.

There was no use in trying to pretend like he wasn't eager to get to the Mossy Glenn. Andy programmed the address into the GPS and saw that it'd take him about half an hour or so to reach the place. He'd get there early, but maybe if he drove slower, looked around and took in the sights, he'd stretch the drive out to about forty-five minutes.

Satisfied he wouldn't be showing up to the Mossy Glenn embarrassingly early, Andy backed out of the parking space. The GPS started rattling off directions and he grimaced. He loved the GPS as much as he hated it. When it worked right, it was great, but sometimes it just spazzed out on him and sent him driving around in circles.

This time, it worked just right. Andy grinned when he saw the gate for the Mossy Glenn. It was open, but above it on a metal arch hung a gorgeous sign for the place. Along with the name of it, there was the iconic shadowed scene of a cowboy on his mount, carrying a calf. The sun was setting over a mountain in the background.

Andy pulled through the gate and began the drive down the long, winding dirt drive. After a few miles, he parked beside a truck in front of the big ranch house. There were several buildings on the land, barns, bunkhouses, equipment sheds, feed storage— all of them looked old but well-maintained with coats of fresh paint. The fencing had been in good shape, too, he'd noted as he drove along.

He unbuckled and got out his briefcase. Inside he had scientific proof of why his company's formulas were the best. He had years of research to back it up, and Andy truly believed in his products. Hell, he'd spent most of his adult life working on them. He wouldn't have done so had he not thought they were the best option and something direly needed.

There were too many chemicals in animals' food today, and it was crossing over into human food, too. Like there wasn't already enough chemicals and shit in what most people ate. *Pick up just about anything from the store and read the ingredients. More chemicals and shit than actual food in it.*

Assured he had everything together, including his wits in case he did see Salt, Andy got out of the truck. He shut the door and spotted a tall, older man standing on the porch to the ranch house. He knew at a glance it wasn't Salt, but there were some similarities. Both men were older, with dark hair and that stern cowboy look to them.

Andy cleared his throat and headed for the porch, letting an easy smile slide into place. He'd always loved ranches, cowboys… If things had been different, he might have tried to buy a place of his own, but shit had happened and there was no changing it.

Andy took the three steps up to the porch easily. He held out his hand. "I'm Andy, but you likely figured that."

"Carlos." Carlos shook his hand. "Come on in. I run this place for my bosses back in Texas, but they'll listen to what I say. Might even be interested in buying your feed for a ranch down there if you can get it to them. *If* your shit's worth buying."

"It is." Andy kept his tone light but firm. He didn't take any offence, and the prospect of being able to sell Organic Feeds products in Texas? That was a win he definitely wanted. "I can get feed to any place in the U.S. Why don't you let me show you why you should give my company a chance. Ask any questions you want, and I won't push you to make a decision." He could tell Carlos was a hard target, but one who'd be a loyal customer if Andy convinced him that Organic Feeds was the best for his ranch.

Carlos wouldn't tolerate any bullshit, either. Andy was relieved to be able to just share his enthusiasm for his products.

"All right, let's head to the office. Troy and Will should be joining us shortly."

"Troy and Will?" Andy repeated, then asked quickly, "Are they ranch hands or —"

"Partners. That's all you need to know about them," Carlos said in a clipped voice.

Andy didn't get the attitude, but whatever. He followed Carlos inside. The house was painted white on the outside, but inside it was an explosion of colour. At least, that was how Andy thought of it. The interior was painted a warm yellow-gold, but there were bright colours everywhere. The hallway had pictures and paintings hanging up, each framed in some colour of the rainbow. There was a small table and mirror done in a dark red in the hall too, then he saw the living room.

Yellow leather couch and love seat, burgundy recliner, and bright bits of pottery on the end tables. More framed pictures and paintings made the place look very homey and comfortable.

Carlos gestured to the left. "Let me grab us a couple cups of coffee."

"That'd be great," Andy told him, though his bladder was beginning to twinge a bit.

The kitchen was the same, but the short guy at the stove didn't seem quite as friendly as the interior of the house looked. Actually, he was cute enough, but he seemed skittish.

"Drake, this here is Andy Calder, and he's here to tell me why he thinks we should switch to his feed for the horses."

"And the pups," Andy said, bending to scratch a happy, bouncy puppy bounding his way.

"Buddy —" Drake began.

Andy squatted and got an armful of puppy and a face-full of licks. "It's okay with me. I love all animals."

Drake chewed on his bottom lip then nodded. "Okay, but he needs to learn some manners."

Andy thought the pup was just being a pup, but it wasn't his place to speak out. He set his briefcase on the floor and used both hands to love on the squirmy beast for a minute or two.

"Okay, that's enough, Buddy." Drake came over and looped a finger through Buddy's collar. "Come on, time for you to go outside anyway." Drake hesitated, and Andy could see the indecision on his face. He couldn't push Drake, though. The man would probably run off if he did.

Finally Drake met his gaze. "What's special about your pet food?"

Andy smiled and stood up, bringing his briefcase with him. "Well, are you the cook here?" It was a pretty easy guess, considering Drake had been cooking something that smelt incredible when they came into the kitchen.

"Yeah, I am." Drake glanced back at the pot on the stove. "I have to put Buddy out. It's his potty time."

Andy nodded. "Speaking of which, may I use your restroom? Preferably inside," he added, winking at Drake.

Drake turned red and Carlos grunted. "He's taken."

Andy turned to Carlos. "I wasn't flirting. I'm about to bust."

Carlos pointed down the hall. "Second door on the right. I'll meet you in the office right across from it. You want cream or sugar?"

Andy shook his head. "Black's fine, thank you." He looked at Drake. "I'm sorry I made you uncomfortable. I tend to be the friendly sort, but not *that* friendly."

"It's fine." Drake hustled away with Buddy in his arms.

Andy sighed and headed for the restroom. He needed to try harder not to piss off or offend anyone here.

After relieving his bladder and washing his hands, Andy met Carlos in the office. Well, not just Carlos. Andy instantly picked up on the connection between Carlos and the other two men. He revised his definition of 'partners' as Carlos had used it earlier. Obviously, he'd meant it as more than just a working term.

"Andy, this is Will." Carlos nodded to the shorter, pretty man with the hazel-green eyes. "And this one here is Troy." Troy was big, broad and bald. He looked like a bouncer, and not someone to mess around with.

Still, Troy's handshake was firm, his smile friendly. Will seemed almost flirtatious, but Andy thought it was likely just his gregarious nature.

Andy laid out the diagrams, the tests and studies done over almost a decade. He explained how the hormones and antibiotics affected not only the animals they were fed to, but also the humans that consumed the meat.

Then he explained how that affected the human body. By the time he was talking about pesticides and genetically modified foods, Drake had been called in and all four of his listeners looked a little grossed out.

"Lots of people don't realise just what it is they're eating, even when they go vegan," Andy added.

Drake rubbed his chin. "I don't know if I can ever cook corn again."

"We can grow our own," Will said, hopping up off the edge of the desk. "I've been telling Carlos and Troy I want a garden."

"And what Will wants, Will gets." Troy hooked an arm around Will's waist and pulled him close. "Right, Carlos?"

Carlos gave Troy and Will an intense look before turning it on Andy. Andy shrugged. "I'da had to be brain-dead not to figure out what was going on with you three." He didn't care. Sure, it was probably hot, really hot, but he hadn't managed a relationship with one man, so two was unfathomable for him.

"Rocky mentioned you were family," Carlos said. "How'd she know that?"

Huh. Guess they don't know about me and Salt. Andy didn't know if mentioning him would cause the man any problems, or cost him a potential customer. Not mentioning him seemed dishonest, though.

Carlos narrowed his eyes and all four men looked at him. Andy hoped he didn't blow it for him or Salt. "Well, I saw this sexy cowboy walk into the feed store in town, and I'm not one to resist temptation when it looks like Salt."

Drake blinked like he was shocked, but the other three men seemed pleased. Andy was relieved they didn't quiz him on whether or not he'd hooked up with Salt. At least they respected his privacy.

"How exactly did you get started in this feed business?" Carlos asked him. "You have all these studies and graphs and such going back over a decade. You aren't old and I have to wonder how you paid for these things"—Carlos tapped some of the papers—"when you'd have had to be pretty damn wealthy to do so."

Andy stood and took one of the papers. He pointed to the name of the doctor who'd written it. "This was my brother, Destry. He passed away from pancreatic cancer a year ago. He was a genius, you know, one of those off-the-charts smart people. He had grants and funding for anything he wanted to do. Just about." There'd been nothing to save his life. Nothing to fix the other problems Destry had had before he'd developed cancer, either.

"I'm sorry for your loss," Carlos murmured, the others adding their condolences too.

"Thank you, but it's been a year, and..." And it still hurt like a fucking mother, but there wasn't anything to be done about it. "And it's good to be following his dream, too. Destry had a lot of physical problems, many of which he attributed to poisons and chemicals he'd ingested in his diet. Granted, lots of people eat the same thing. His theory was, though, that some people are more sensitive to chemicals, and that we'd be seeing a cataclysmic rise in diseases such as cancer because of our contaminated food sources."

Andy sat back down. "Now, I'm not saying that's the case, but I can't say it isn't, either, and after watching everything my brother went through, I am probably more on the paranoid side than not nowadays. I can't help but think that Nature has its way, and tampering with that lands us in deep shit.

"And I went to college with a couple of guys who were health nuts," he continued. "Smart, too, though maybe not quite up there with Destry. They've contributed too, and not just on paper. They've invested a good chunk of money in our company because they believe in what we're doing. You'll find all the company information in that Organics Feed packet right there on the desk.

"If you have any questions, you can call me, or my other brother, Brandt, who is co-owner. His numbers and e-mail addresses are in that packet too. He's a good guy, but he does have a family." And saying that caused a twinge of pain in Andy's chest. "So I'd ask you not to call past ten at night, generally."

"That's just being courteous anyhow, family or no," Troy said. "I was raised not to be calling people at all hours unless there was an emergency."

Andy felt his lopsided grin slip into place. "Well now, there's some folks who think a hangnail is an emergency."

Will rolled his eyes and Troy snorted. Will muttered something about divas needing to learn some manners, but Andy didn't think those words were for him and so he didn't comment.

"I'm going to go finish getting lunch ready," Drake told them. He glanced at Andy. "You're welcome to stay. Salt should be coming up to eat." Then he smirked and his entire face lit up before he turned and left the room.

"Someone's playing matchmaker," Will crooned, clapping his hands. "I was gonna do it, but since Drake did, I guess I can step back and let him take the credit if you and Salt hit it off."

But Troy cocked his head and looked at Andy. "I overheard one of the guys teasing Salt yesterday about a hot date."

Andy shook his head and kept his grin in place. "Sorry, I'm going to go wash up and thank Drake for the lunch invite. I think I'll join you, if that's okay?"

Carlos laughed and Troy frowned. Will looked like he was up to something, but they all told him he was welcome. Andy stood. "Okay then. If you have any questions or concerns, let me know. Of course, if you'd like to order, let me know that, too. I have some samples in the truck, including a bag of the best puppy food on the planet."

After he went and got the bag out of the truck bed, Andy returned inside and set the dog food by the door. He stopped by the kitchen to let Drake know it was there, then he washed up in the restroom.

When he turned the water off, his belly gave a flop and he had the strangest sensation, as if he were about to swoon—all because he heard Salt's voice, the already familiar cadence of his laughter.

Andy wasn't sure that staying for lunch had been wise after all. But he damned well wanted another night with Salt.

Chapter Five

Jesus, it was one of those days where time just dragged its ass like someone had tacked on a two-ton weight to it. Maybe if Salt hadn't seen that red truck pull up, if he hadn't caught a glimpse of Andy getting out of it, the morning would have passed quicker.

It took all of Salt's restraint to keep from finding excuses to go up to the ranch house. He did every job he needed to get done, some of his afternoon stuff, too. When lunch time came around and he rode back into the yard, that red truck was still there and Salt just about whooped for joy.

Goddamn, he was happy to see that vehicle!

Salt got the tack off his horse and brushed her down in record time. He had Ramsey put her up and handle the feed—that newbie needed a serious attitude adjustment. Ramsey was going to figure out that working on one ranch for a few years didn't make him knowledgeable about every damn thing a cowboy needed to know.

Salt jogged over to the bunkhouse and took a few minutes to wash his face and hands. He brushed his teeth, too, because it seemed like a good idea. Of course, Drake would probably fix something garlicky, but as long as Andy ate it, too…

Salt harrumphed at himself and wiped a splotch of toothpaste off his chin. Like he was going to be jumping on Andy any time soon. Andy might not even give a shit about seeing Salt again. At least Salt wasn't worried that Andy was only interested in him as a means to sell to the Mossy G. Andy had approached him before he knew where Salt worked.

Regardless of the what-if's and possible rejection, Salt was still happy as a kid on Christmas when he walked into the big house. Will greeted him by singing about Salt and someone sitting in the tree. Salt laughed and shook his head.

"You're putting way more into it than what it is," Salt told Will. "He's gonna be moving on."

Will scrunched up his face and crossed his arms over his chest. "Don't be a dick." Then just as quickly, he groaned and smacked his own forehead. "Oh, ignore me. There's not a damn thing wrong with just having some fun."

"You've got that happy couples…er, threesome thing going on," Salt informed him. "You want everyone to be just as happy as you three are, but sometimes that ain't meant for everyone. Some of us might just have to settle for what we can get."

About that time, Salt saw Andy coming out of the hall bathroom. Andy saw him, too, and any doubt Salt had about Andy wanting to hook up with him again vanished. He'd have sworn an electrical current of sexual desire crackled in the air between them, and for one split second, Salt couldn't hear anything but the sound of his heartbeat.

Then the noise of cowhands talking and laughing came roaring back in. Salt heard Will tell him to go have a seat, and he was walking before he knew it. Andy was headed his way, never glancing aside.

Not until Troy tapped him on the shoulder and pointed to a chair. A chair right beside Salt's usual seat. Salt scooted around a couple of people and finally reached his spot. Andy looked up at him, grinning like he'd never been happy before that moment.

Salt's heart thudded heavily and he wondered if his blood had been infused with helium. He thought he could just about float off, but he didn't. Instead he murmured a hello to Andy, then pulled out his chair and sat beside the sexy man.

"You smell like sunshine and hard work, horse and leather," Andy whispered in his ear. "God, you have no idea how bad I want to fuck you."

The words were so softly spoken, Salt had to strain to hear them, and it was that softness, combined with the words themselves, that caused a rapid reaction from Salt's dick. He winced as his filling pecker was pinched in a fold of his jeans. Salt inhaled and the citrus and smoke scent of Andy's cologne filled his nostrils.

He had to shift in his seat and bob his head in agreement. It took him a couple of tries to speak past the lump of need in his throat. "I want that too."

Andy pressed his knee to Salt's. Then he moved closer until his outer thigh was against Salt's. "Been working hard?" Andy asked, sounding for all the world as if he wasn't so hard and horny he was ready to crack.

Maybe he wasn't, but Salt was considering grabbing him and dragging him back to that bathroom. "Yeah,

yeah, been keeping busy." He looked into Andy's dark eyes and the truth just fell from his lips. "I knew you were here and had to force myself to stay away. Damn near finished all my work for the day."

"You should take the afternoon off then," Will said, sliding into the seat beside Salt. "Seriously. I smell the horny coming off you both."

Everyone in the room went silent. Salt sighed and closed his eyes. "Will."

"Isn't that like sexual harassment?" Troy asked. "Look, Salt's blushing."

"Maybe I should go," Andy offered.

Salt opened his eyes and grabbed the man's knee under the table. "No, they don't mean anything by it. They're just teasing."

"I have this problem with my foot," Will began, sounding morose. "It just keeps flying up and filling my mouth. Sorry, guys."

"God, ain't that the truth," Carlos added. "Of course, that makes you special, in a good way. Wouldn't change a thing about you."

Will glared at Carlos then he stuck his tongue out at him. "Whatever. Let's eat."

And that simply, the awkwardness was gone. Salt kept his hand on Andy's knee, just because it felt good, and it wasn't like there was a secret to be kept.

"You got plans for the rest of the day?" he asked Andy in between bites of the best damn enchiladas on the planet.

Andy shook his head, his mouth full of cheesy goodness.

"Want some company?"

Andy swallowed quickly. "Hell yeah."

Salt smirked. "Yeah, I think Will owes me an afternoon off for his earlier blabbering."

Will popped Salt on the arm. "I wasn't joking. Carlos had already told me you could take off."

Salt looked at Carlos, who kind of grimaced as he spoke. "I thought you've been working hard for the past few months, and not taking more than a day off here and there. You need to at least have a full day or two off every week."

Salt had been busy helping to get the ranch in shape, and it wasn't like he'd had other stuff to do before. Before today, or last night.

"Nah, I'll finish up with my stuff, and leave early if I get done early." As much as he wanted Andy, Salt couldn't just shrug off his work. That wasn't how he was made. He shot Andy an apologetic look, but Andy didn't look irritated. No, the man looked downright pleased as if he was proud of Salt for making them both wait.

"A good work ethic turns me on," Andy said quietly, but not quietly enough because Will snickered.

"Well then, Salt should be making you hor —"

"Will," Troy growled, and Will beamed at the bald man.

Someone else besides Salt was going to be getting fucked good and hard tonight. Andy gave Salt's balls a little squeeze then left off tormenting him to resume eating.

As much as Salt loved those enchiladas, they suddenly tasted like dust in his mouth. Desire pinged throughout his body, making him ache with a sweet need that he wanted to revel in.

"Is everyone usually so friendly here?"

Salt glanced at Ramsey, who shrugged and stuffed a forkful of food into his mouth. "Jush wondered," Ramsey said around his fork.

Carlos canted his head and studied Ramsey. "If by friendly, you mean do people joke and flirt a little? Yeah, they're allowed to do that. Working on a ranch and living together makes for some close relationships, and not all of them are private, or strictly companionable. I'd think you'd know that, having worked on a ranch before."

Ramsey ducked his head and didn't say another word, but Salt started paying more attention to the man. Something about Ramsey had seemed off to Salt from the start. His lack of knowledge in regards to his job, for one thing. It was like he knew what the job entailed because he'd memorised it, or played at it. But Carlos had surely checked his references. Maybe the guy was just weird. It happened.

But Salt was going to be keeping a closer eye on him from now on.

* * * *

It was odd, how comfortable he felt there with the Mossy Glenn crew. Andy hadn't expected it, but it was almost like having a second home. He was teased by the folks there almost as much as he was by his brothers. Andy liked it.

He liked it enough that he didn't leave after lunch, but let Will give him a tour of the buildings nearby, then Carlos took him out to see some of the land. Andy's ass and thighs were going to regret him riding horseback for the first time in years, but the rest of him enjoyed the hell out of it, and Carlos was surprisingly good company.

At least, that was Andy's opinion until they pulled their mounts up under a gorgeous shade tree. Across a pasture, Andy could see a couple of riders herding horses for reasons unbeknownst to him. It didn't matter, because one of those figures was tall and lean, sitting proud in the saddle. Andy's pulse danced and he actually had to press a hand to his chest when his heart fluttered madly.

He'd forgotten that Carlos was even there while Andy had been staring at Salt. Then Carlos spoke and pulled Andy right out of his lusty daze.

"He's a good man," Carlos rumbled. "Reminds me of a nicer version of me."

Andy slanted Carlos a quick look before returning his gaze to Salt. "Nicer? You seem all right to me."

Carlos grunted. Andy looked at him again and Carlos tipped his hat up an inch or so. "Salt has an easy laugh, easy smile and maybe just an easy personality, but that don't mean he's shallow. I think that's mostly a cover to keep himself from being hurt. It's a hard row to hoe, being a gay cowboy out here. He's had decades of having to hide who he really is. I know for a fact that can do something to a man, make him think less of himself because inside, you feel you've lied all your life."

Andy held up a hand. "Whoa. You're getting deep on me, Carlos. I don't even know Salt, not really." He just knew how Salt sounded, how he looked when he came. How Salt's smile seemed to reach in and grab him—"I've got other places to be after this, too. We're just getting the company up and running, and there's millions of dollars at stake."

Carlos grimaced and his expression shuttered. "Yeah, well. Money doesn't mean shit when that's all you got." He put his fingers in his mouth and whistled so loud Andy thought his ears were going to bleed.

Andy couldn't help but think it was punishment for something Carlos thought he'd done wrong, especially when Carlos smirked.

Dick. Andy rubbed one ear and Carlos looked plumb pleased. "Salt don't deserve to be treated like a piece of ass."

Well, now he knew why Carlos was being a pissy bitch. Andy sat up a little straighter. "What Salt and I do together isn't your business. You don't know what he wants, I'd wager money on that." Shit, it wasn't like he and Salt had traded class rings—they weren't dumb kids. They were adults, who knew the reality of life and especially life as a gay man where they lived.

Yeah, Salt worked on an LGBTQ-supportive ranch, but that kind of acceptance sure didn't extend to the rest of the cowboy world. Andy knew there'd be more lost sales should he wave a rainbow flag out in the open. There were many people depending on him now, friends, family, and both were investors in the business.

Carlos was glaring at him and Andy met him with a level stare of his own. "You might be Salt's friend, you might be more employer than anything else. Either way, you do him a disservice by trying to interfere on his behalf. Salt is an intelligent man, and he knows damn well that I'll be leaving."

Okay, they hadn't discussed it exactly in those terms, but both of them were old enough and experienced enough to know what the deal was. It wouldn't hurt to clarify it, just to be safe, though.

Carlos opened his mouth to retort something probably not very nice, Andy would guess, but Salt came riding over, a lazy grin on his face. "Hey now, y'all can't just come and stare. You ride out, you get put to work."

"I thought you were finishing up early?" Andy asked, suddenly aching to be alone with Salt.

Salt gestured over his shoulder with his thumb. "Yeah, that was the plan, but Ramsey isn't as skilled as he should be and that's slowing me down."

Carlos frowned, deep lines etching around his mouth. "What do you mean he isn't as skilled as he should be? His references checked out. He worked at the JHL Ranch for over three years."

Salt shook his head. "Then they must not have had him doing more than mucking stalls. He can't lasso for shit, and every time I tell him to cut his mount one way, he hesitates and half the time goes the opposite." Salt shrugged. "Maybe it's the heat. God knows it's melting my brain."

"Or maybe he's a liar," Carlos growled. "Go on, Salt. I'm gonna work with Ramsey. You tell Troy and Will where I am, okay? Then get gone."

Andy half-expected Carlos to add some withering comment about Salt and Andy not having much time before Andy split, but he didn't. Andy couldn't tell if Carlos didn't like him, or was just worried about Salt. He thought it was the latter, because Carlos had been friendly up until they'd stopped a few minutes ago.

Salt took off his hat and used a bandana to wipe his sweaty brow. His hair was damp and his shirt was too, soaked in spots from working outside on such a hot day.

Andy wanted to strip him right there and roll all over him, covering himself in the scent of musky, sweaty man. He settled for snatching the bandana from Salt's hand and tucking it in his own back pocket.

"Hey! That's wet and—"

"And coated in one of my favourite smells," Andy interrupted. He waggled his eyebrows. "Damn, man, you have no idea how much I want to just bury my face in your ass and breathe you in."

Salt's sharp inhale and the way his pupils expanded didn't help Andy to repress that desire one bit. "Come on," Andy rasped. "Let's get back so I can get you naked and fuck you until your throat's so raw from screaming my name you can't even whimper."

"Jesus, the things you say," Salt got out in a stripped voice. He clucked and his horse took off at a full run.

Andy whooped and was right on his tail.

Chapter Six

Andy had apparently meant it when he'd said that bandana held one of his favourite scents. Salt barely got into the hotel room before Andy tackled him, a full-body lunge that knocked the breath out of him and sent them both sprawling onto the bed. Salt gasped, meaning to take in some air, but what he got was Andy gripping his face, his hair, and taking his mouth in a forceful kiss that pushed a mewling sound right out of Salt.

They scrambled to get each other's clothes off, twisting, shoving, tearing, even. Salt heard a rip, didn't know if it was his shirt or Andy's. He didn't much care, either. Andy's hot mouth on his throat was pure bliss, the scrape of his teeth a perfection of sensation that had Salt bucking up, driving his steel-hard cock against Andy's.

Andy bit him, sucked and scraped Salt's skin with his teeth. He held Salt by the jaw, nipping his way down to teeth Salt's nipples.

Salt was going to lose his ever-lovin' mind. "Please," he gasped, writhing as his cock spurted pre-cum.

Andy's response was a perfectly vicious bite that had Salt shouting and clutching Andy's head to his chest. Andy worked Salt's nipple until that little pinpoint of flesh throbbed with each heartbeat, then he pulled back and flipped Salt onto his belly.

Somewhere along the way, Salt's belt had been unfastened. Andy had Salt's jeans and briefs down in seconds. He grabbed Salt by the shoulder and hip. "Come here."

The command had Salt scooting, but with his pants and underwear down around his knees, and his boots still on, his movement was limited. That was okay, because Andy man-handled him around until his knees were on the floor and he was bent over the side of the bed.

Andy slapped Salt's ass and before Salt could tell him he didn't like that kind of rough play, pleasure bloomed hot and bright in Salt's ass. It spread out from that handprint until it was burrowed deep in his gut, warming him all over.

Salt couldn't process the why of that. His experiences at a leather club he'd braved some years back had purely sucked. Pain hadn't been something he'd been able to enjoy, yet he found himself begging. "More. Do it again."

Andy's breathless laugh came right before another, harder, slap to Salt's ass. Salt moaned and closed his eyes, embarrassed and needy in a way he hadn't ever been before. A third and fourth slap followed, setting his skin on fire, then Andy prised his cheeks apart.

Salt's eyes snapped open. "Andy, I been working— oh my fucking God!" Salt squeaked immediately after shouting. Andy's tongue was hot, wet, perfect as Andy licked down Salt's crease.

Andy rumbled, sounding for all the world like he was enjoying what he was doing, so Salt shut up, except for the soft moans and curses that he couldn't hold back. Andy squeezed Salt's cheeks hard, marking his paler flesh, Salt hoped. He tried to arch, to wiggle his ass back for more. Andy smacked his butt again, then pinched it, and Salt had to shove a hand under himself to fist his dick and try to stem his impending climax.

It took more of a thump than a grip, but Salt got himself under control. He almost lost it again when Andy tongued his asshole. Andy reached around and flicked the tip of Salt's shaft. That made him howl, and not entirely with pain. Jesus, Andy was driving him nuts. There wasn't a part of Salt that didn't feel screamingly alive and thrumming with the need for Andy to fuck him.

The press of Andy's tongue into his hole was magical, perfect and dirty and oh so right. Salt raised his head up and thumped it against the mattress a few times, pushing back against Andy's face. He was going to go insane, just screaming, bat-shit crazy if Andy didn't fuck him soon.

Andy ran his other hand down Salt's ass to the back of his thigh. He landed a smack there that drove something close to a sob out of Salt. It wasn't the pain, but the way Andy seemed to know what Salt needed, even when Salt himself hadn't had a clue. Well, he'd had a clue, hence the visit to the leather club, but… But that had been years ago, when he'd thought all he'd ever have were one-offs with strangers.

He knew Andy, even if it was just barely. It was still more than Salt had experienced with any other man. It sure seemed like Andy knew him, too.

Andy pushed what had to be at least two fingers into Salt's ass and Salt quit thinking of anything but the way that stretch and burn made him feel. He wished he could part his legs, wished he had more freedom of movement, but there was something extremely hot about being unable to do more than squirm, too.

Plus, if Andy fucked him like that, his ass would be squeezing Andy's dick so tight it might just blow Andy's mind.

Andy thrust those fingers in hard and fast. "You can take it, right? Take it rough, cowboy?"

"Yeah," Salt managed to get out. He was reeling just a bit from discovering that he did and could want it rough, but later he'd analyse that. *Or not.*

"Fucking perfect," Andy told him. Another finger was worked into him and Salt panted his way through it. He hadn't had anything up his ass, not even his own fingers, in a few years. Maybe even longer. Usually, he'd topped on the few occasions anal sex had happened. Seemed to be expected of him. There'd been a time or two he'd bottomed — like at the leather club. He'd liked it, thought he could love it if given the chance, but hadn't been given the opportunity.

Until Andy. He'd wanted Andy to fuck him since he'd first seen the man.

Andy wasn't gentle prepping Salt, and Salt was damned glad. He'd have been offended to be treated like he was fragile, and he was learning new things about himself every time Andy shoved those fingers in deep.

Then Andy touched his prostate, just a whisper of contact, and Salt's eyes whipped open as he jolted. "Again!"

Andy slapped his hip. "Bossy." But he did it again and Salt began to tremble with the force of holding himself back.

Andy purred and slapped Salt's cock. "Hold on, cowboy."

Pain shot down Salt's length, but oddly enough, it didn't make him go soft, not at all. If anything, his dick got even harder. He was dimly aware of Andy cursing, then those fingers were gone, leaving Salt empty. He started to raise his head up and protest, but the sound of a condom wrapper being torn open shut him up.

There was the cool, runny feel of lube sliding down his crease, then Andy was back to fingering his hole, working the slick stuff inside him. It only took a minute, then Andy withdrew his fingers and settled behind Salt. He reached under Salt again and clutched the tip of his dick. Andy squeezed it, at the same time lining his fat cock up to Salt's hole.

When Andy thumbed Salt's slit, he also thrust, pushing fully into Salt's ass. It was a quick, sharp piercing pain that tore through Salt, then pleasure saturated him as wholly as possible. He keened and tried to arch, but Andy bent over him and began pounding into him, short, hard thrusts, long, deep ones — there was no particular rhythm, as if Andy just gave way to his body's needs.

He kept working the tip of Salt's dick with a lube-slicked hand, too. Salt clawed at the bedcovers as he was fucked wildly. He felt the scrape of teeth over his nape at the same time Andy pushed a fingertip hard against his slit.

Salt's balls drew tight. He clenched all over, his ass grabbing greedily at Andy's shaft. Andy bellowed and hammered into him harder, the bed squeaking in protest as Salt was rammed against it repeatedly. The moan that left him sounded almost unworldly, but the ecstasy that was flooding him seemed unworldly too.

Andy bit him harder, and Salt came so hard and fast he couldn't breathe, couldn't scream. He was so dizzy it seemed like the entire world tipped and tilted. Andy's pressure to Salt's slit just made the spunk pour out of Salt.

Andy shouted and drove in with even greater force. He slammed in another half dozen times then stilled for a split second as the first pulse of his cum shot into the condom. Then he ground his hips against Salt's ass through a few more jets of his release.

And finally, Andy sighed and collapsed on top of him. His rough panting matched Salt's as they lay there for a moment.

"Damn, got to move," Andy groaned. "God…"

Salt winced when Andy withdrew his dick. Salt's hole was definitely tender and sore. He felt well-fucked, and worn out. Kind of like he'd never move again. Hell, he couldn't even open his eyes.

The sound of Andy's uneven footsteps made him grin. He wasn't the only one who was fucked out. Salt squirmed and got his pants and underwear back up over his ass, then he pushed up enough to get himself sprawled on the bed. He was asleep before Andy ever even came back out of the bathroom.

* * * *

What the hell just happened? Andy leaned over the toilet with a hand against the wall as he took a piss. He was shaken to the soles of his feet by the intensity of what he and Salt had just done. *And smacking the guy's ass and dick? Shit. Shit!* There was no doubt that

Salt had liked it. The man had come buckets—well, he'd come a lot anyways. Andy was fairly certain Salt wasn't used to some of the stuff Andy had just done to him.

Fucking among them. Salt's ass had been tighter than a banker's purse strings. It'd driven Andy to the point of desperation, feeling those tight inner walls clenching, the fierce grip of Salt's ring around his fingers, his cock, his tongue.

And hell's bells, Salt had tasted fucking divine. All man and sweat, it was one of Andy's kinks, to be sure. It was a rare treat, because most of his hookups smelt like freshly showered male, not hard-working, rough, tough cowboy.

Andy groaned as his dick twitched. He shook it off and flushed the toilet. Man, he was forever going to carry the image of Salt shoved down over that bed, his ass red, that tight, tight hole clinging around Andy's dick. Never had Andy seen such an erotic sight.

Never had he felt such pleasure. Almost crushing, really, because he was close to panicking over it.

He didn't want strings.

But he didn't want to never see Salt again, never fuck the man's ass or mouth again. Never see that smile or the way Salt's eyes lit up when he was having fun, or the way they went hazy when he was feeling lusty. Didn't want to never sit and talk with him like they'd done the night before.

Andy pressed a hand against his stomach. He was a damned mess. That was what he was.

After he pulled up his pants and underwear, and tucked his cock away, Andy washed his hands and face. He felt inexplicably nervous, as if he'd never talked to Salt before. Like he was going to walk back into the room, and a stranger would be in there waiting for him.

A glance in the mirror told him a different story. He didn't recognise the man looking back at him, flushed with the evidence of his orgasm, lips swollen from kisses, from rimming Salt's ass, from biting his own lips as he pounded away at Salt's hole. Sated—even through the worry, Andy could see that he was sated, content and not in any hurry to pack his shit and run.

Like I always do. But Salt's been an anomaly all this time. He's the only man I've cared to have two nights with, even if he won't actually stay the night. At least since college, anyway.

Maybe that was just because he hadn't got to fuck Salt the night before. And because Salt had been the one to sneak off.

Not sneak off. Andy shook his head and turned away from the mirror. Salt had left like all good one-night stands should do. Go without bitching and moaning or waking Andy up.

God, he was an asshole.

Andy swiped a hand over his chin. He was stalling, and that was dumb. Salt didn't expect anything from him other than what he'd just got.

It still wouldn't hurt to make sure Salt knew that. They'd have a little chat, as soon as Andy stepped back into the room. And who knew? Maybe they'd come to some kind of arrangement. It'd maybe be cool to have a guy he'd be able to hook up with when he was in the area. Be beneficial for them both, because Salt seemed like he'd enjoyed the fuck out of what they'd done.

Mind made up, Andy opened the bedroom door, mouth open to start yapping. The vision Salt made, sprawled on the bed, his pants pulled up almost fully but not quite, so that Andy could see the furrow of his crack, his lips parted, face relaxed in slumber… Andy closed his mouth. There was that weird racing of his pulse again, that warm wiggly feeling in his chest.

He'd get a checkup tomorrow. That sensation was disturbing him, but for now, he wanted to go get in bed with Salt, maybe sleep with him and wake up in a few hours so they could fuck again.

That was all Andy meant to do. He couldn't say why he stripped to his boxer briefs and crawled carefully onto the bed before curling up beside Salt. He couldn't explain why he experienced a gush of warmth inside, like some romantic greeting card commercial had come to life inside him.

And he couldn't explain, nor did he care to examine, why the soft snuffling sound Salt made was music to his ears. Or why it had Andy scooting closer, closing his eyes and drifting off to sleep.

Chapter Seven

For the second night in a row, Salt woke up with Andy beside him. It took him a few minutes to figure that out, of course. He wasn't always quick on the uptake when just waking.

The hotel room was dark, too, with only a bit of light coming from beneath the bathroom door. Salt's tender ass brought to mind exactly what had happened between him and Andy earlier.

It was kind of embarrassing, Salt decided. He'd let someone slap his ass, slap his dick, and he'd come like he'd stored up a year's worth of jizz in his balls. He'd *liked* the pain, because it hadn't been pain, exactly. It'd...it'd been more than that one singular sensation.

Salt still didn't know that he wanted to face Andy, though. He'd let the man hit him, for Christ's sake. And yeah, yeah, he'd been in a leather club looking into something like that. But he'd hated it. That was probably an understatement, even.

Salt couldn't figure it out when he was sleep-addled, sore-assed and starving. It probably didn't even matter, because Andy would be moving on soon. He had a business to build and all that shit.

Thinking about that had Salt easing off the bed. He was already a mess over the man, or at least over what had happened between them. *Maybe not a mess, but I got some thinking to do for sure.*

"Running out on me again?"

Salt froze upon hearing Andy's voice. Did the man sound mad? Salt twisted around, even though he could barely make out Andy's features in the darkness. "Got to piss, and I didn't figure you'd have need of me now."

Shit, did *he* sound mad? Salt cleared his throat. It was just that he'd been sleeping and had that growly just-woke-up thing going on. Probably the same for Andy.

Andy sat up and turned the bedside lamp on, which just about blinded Salt. "Shit, warn a man, will ya?" He blinked and ignored the spike of pain in his right temple.

"Sorry." Andy sounded more amused than sorry, but Salt let it go. "That's what you get for trying to sneak away."

Salt blinked faster and glared. "What the hell are you talking about?"

"Fuck. I don't even know." Andy ran his hands over his face, then fisted them in his hair, pulling so hard his eyes tilted and his brows arched. "Man, I don't fucking know."

Salt was concerned at Andy's obvious distress. "Hey, no reason to worry. You just woke up. We're both kind of addle-brained from sleep."

Andy shook his head. "No. No, that isn't it. I don't know. Maybe it is."

Salt leant back, watching Andy closely. He didn't know the man well after all, and maybe he was unstable or something.

Andy looked at him and scoffed, "Stop it. I'm not fucking crazy."

"If you say so." Salt finished standing up and looked around for his keys. He hadn't got far in the door before Andy had pounced on him, and he hadn't put the keys in his pocket. He was going to have to turn the rest of the lights on so he could see.

"I'm not. Asshole." Andy got up too, and the sight of all that soft, tanned skin caused Salt to pause. Andy had a fantastic ass, too, all round and plump and—"I just, I'm—" Andy huffed and looked like he was about to stomp his foot. Instead he faced Salt, and the confusion in the man's expression was kind of heart wrenching. "I'm just not sure we should be done with each other." He smiled nervously. "I mean, I'd... I'd like you to stay for a few hours longer, if you can, instead of running out of here like a cheap trick."

Salt arched a brow at Andy. "You always wake up being a dick? Because if so, I gotta say I wish I'd gotten out of here earlier."

Andy blushed and his lips thinned. Salt figured that was that, then, because he wasn't the kind to play games and Andy was swinging hot and cold or friendly and bitchy, something. Salt wasn't going to hang around to figure it out.

He walked over to the switches beside the door and flipped them up, turning on the overhead lights. He spotted his keys under the little table by the window.

"I'm sorry." Andy came over, approaching him slowly. "I am, okay?"

Salt looked him in the eyes. Andy was blushing so dark he looked in danger of keeling over. "I guess my pride got hurt," Andy muttered. "You snuck off—Sorry, sorry. You left without waking me up last night, and I woke up and wished..." Andy took a deep, stuttery breath. "Shit, this is hard."

Salt was getting a completely uncalled-for surge of hope trying to come hopping to life in him. *No*, he told himself. *Stop it. Just cause I'm a lonely old cuss don't mean Andy wants more than a fuck or two.*

Andy held out a hand then brought it back to clutch it nervously in his other. "God damn, I just think maybe it'd be nice to wake up and not have you hightailin' it away like you can't wait to get away from me."

Well, that about crushed that budding hope. Salt walked to the table and squatted. He grabbed his keys as he spoke. "Andy, I surely don't know what bug crawled up your ass when you fell asleep, but I hope it comes back out and you quit acting like a fuckhead." Salt didn't know why he felt hurt. It was stupid, but he couldn't help it. "You keep taking pot shots at me, well, fuck you. Just because I let you fuck me and slap my ass" —*and dick, Jesus* —"don't mean you can treat me like shit."

Like the guy at the leather club.

Salt stood and Andy was staring at the floor, or his feet, Salt didn't know and didn't fucking care. He just wanted his own bed. "You're not the first guy who's done that. I thought you were better than the other, though. Guess I was wrong."

Salt pushed past Andy and opened the motel door. He wanted to hear Andy call him back, but he didn't. He stepped through the door—and stopped at the soft touch to his shoulder.

"Please don't," Andy said quietly. "You're right. I'm being a dick. I... Please come back in and shut the door. Please. If I'm an asshole again, you can knock the bullshit out of me. I won't even swing back."

Salt sighed to himself. He went back into the motel room. Why, he couldn't say, but walking away just seemed wrong. Andy backed up and sat in one of the chairs at the table. He nibbled on his lip and watched Salt.

What was he supposed to do? Salt settled for sitting in the other chair. Andy left off trying to chew his lip off and put his hands on the table. "The thing is," he began, nervousness evident in his voice. "I don't do relationships. I couldn't, before. I had responsibilities that I've since been relieved of —"

And doesn't he sound bitter about it? Salt wondered why.

"And with the company, you know how people are. They find out I'm gay and there'll be more sales lost than made." Andy shook his head. "I just don't know how to be out-out. I took a chance in the feed store, because you're just that fucking irresistible. I haven't been with the same man twice like I have with you, not in a long long time, and the thing is..." Andy sat up and took another deep breath. He seemed to have to force himself to meet Salt's gaze.

"The thing is, I don't want to not do this again." Andy waved at the bed. "Not just that, not just fucking, you know? I liked talking to you. I liked eating lunch with you at the ranch, and...and just hanging around you. That freaked me out. So I was a total dick, but I don't—maybe if we do this all a few more times, I won't want to see you again. I don't know. I don't know what you want, either."

Salt was trying to process that jumbled mess of a confession. He frowned and rubbed his temple as that throbbing started up again. "Wait. You want what? To be fuck buddies?"

"Maybe?" Andy asked. "Does that piss you off?"

Salt almost laughed at that. "Hell no. I'm not averse to that, Andy. I've never had a steady anything, so yeah, I get the confusion. Might want to try not being a jackass next time you're feeling that way over something. Easier to just talk it out and then you don't have to apologise."

Andy grinned. "Okay. You're…you're good with us hooking up when I'm in the area? No strings?"

Salt ignored the little voice in his head that protested that. "Yeah, I am." Hell, it was more than he'd ever had before. And, he liked Andy, when he wasn't waking up and being an idiot.

Andy beamed at him, his entire face brightening. "Cool. Awesome. So what was that about some other guy smacking your ass?"

"Shoulda known you were gonna come back to that," Salt griped, but he had been the one to bring it up. "See, years back, I was in between jobs for a few days. I saw an ad online for this leather club in Helena. I was horny, figured it'd be a good, easy place to get fucked and maybe see what all the BDSM fuss was about. I was curious." He laughed at his naïvety. "Man, I bought this leather jockstrap." He shook his head. God, he'd been such an idiot.

"I bet you were sexy as fuck," Andy said in a voice rough with burgeoning desire. "All long, lean muscles with that tight, tiny ass."

"What ass?" Salt huffed. "Man, I ain't built like you back there."

Andy looked at him like he was crazy. "Seriously? Salt, you have this perfect, lean butt that's so tight it just about squeezed my dick off. Not an ounce of fat on it, just taut, sculpted ass..."

Andy made his backside sound downright attractive. Salt let it go. Andy had seemed to enjoy fucking it earlier. "Anyway, I go there, and sheee-it, there really were men getting whipped, and gang-banged, and fisted. I was just a hick in a place I shouldn't have been. The first night, there was this one guy who kept looking at me. Big, one of those bear types. Older than me, too. He looked brutal and I was not interested in catching his attention any more than I already had."

"The first night?" Andy asked.

Salt nodded. "Yup, I was dumb and horny so I went back the next night. Got a few drinks in me ahead of time to bolster my courage, because it sure seemed like those guys getting whaled on the night before were enjoying it. Made my dick hard seeing it, too. I knew I didn't want to be the one doing the hitting." Salt hitched up a shoulder. It was embarrassing how dumb he'd been. "So I was feeling good when I got there. More outgoing, I guess, with the way alcohol makes you feel ten feet tall sometimes. I wasn't drunk, or don't think I was. Might have been more intoxicated than I realised, looking back on it now. Anyway. This big old bear came up to me and told me to kneel. I did, since everyone seemed to be looking at me then. Figured I'd be kneeling either willingly or not in seconds, so I went down and he proceeded to fuck my mouth right there in front of everyone without so much as a 'Do you wanna'. And before you ask, I did. Want to."

So badly that he'd been mortified by his need.

"There's no shame in wanting to submit." Andy tipped his chin up, as if he was daring Salt to argue.

"Nothing wrong with enjoying pain and being tied up, fucked hard."

"No, I know that," Salt agreed. "I was shocked at how much I liked it. What I didn't like was that he kept calling me names. I just don't get off on that kind of humiliation, I guess. I couldn't get his dick out of my mouth to tell him to shut the fuck up, either. When he pulled out, he came on my face and told me to get on my hands and knees so his buddies could fuck me."

"No," Andy said, eyes rounding.

Salt nodded. "That's what I said, and surprisingly, he listened to that. Seemed he'd been so hard for me—his words—he'd forgotten to talk about safe words and such. We were both fools, but he was supposed to be the experienced Dom. Turns out he was just a wannabe, and I don't want a Dom."

"Was that all?" Andy asked, frowning at him. "Why do I sense more?"

"Because I was drunk and stupid," Salt said blandly. "I let the wannabe talk me into a private room, where he tied me up and tried to cane me."

"Fuck." Andy stood up and Salt waved him back down.

"No, I told him I wanted to try it, and I wanted him to fuck me. Pretty fucking stupid, and let me tell you, a cane fucking hurts." Lord, Salt's ass ached with the memory of it, still. "Two hits with it and I was out of my mind with pain. He left off caning me, and started pushing lube up my ass. At that point, I didn't care if he fucked me, I just wanted it all over with, and I refused to say my safe word because I thought I'd come off as a pussy. That was the longest half hour of my life. Thought he'd never come."

Andy sat back down. He looked like he wanted to say something, and Salt had a fairly good idea of what it was. "Go on, tell me I was stupid and I should have used my safe word."

"He shouldn't have done anything with you, knowing you'd been drinking," Andy began, but Salt waved a hand to cut him off.

"He might not have known. I was drinking vodka, and I'm a pretty undetectable drunk if you don't know me." Salt wasn't a sloppy drunk at all. "Now, I do think he shouldn't have been calling himself a Dom. Everything I've read up on that shit since then tells me he should have been aware of the fact I didn't enjoy anything he did to me. Then again, maybe I'm reading the wrong stuff."

Andy crossed his arms over his chest. "You like me being rough with you."

"A hell of a lot," Salt admitted. "Surprised me, but you weren't brutal, you know. And maybe because I know you a little, it was different."

"I'm not a Dom," Andy said firmly.

"I don't want a Dom." Salt was pretty sure he'd already said as much. "I guess I like the rough sometimes, though. I also don't think I'm going to want to bottom every time, so if that's a problem…"

"It's not. I prefer to top, but sometimes I like a cock up my ass, too." Andy looked at him intently and Salt grunted. He had really liked getting fucked, so as long as he could occasionally swap positions, he was fine with that.

"Are we done negotiating?" Andy finally enquired.

Salt cocked his head. "Was that what we were doing?"

Andy bobbed his head. "Sure. It'd suck to find out we weren't as compatible in the sack as we'd thought we were."

"Yeah, I reckon it would." Salt fidgeted with his wrist. He hadn't even bothered finding his shirt, he realised.

"Anything else before I drag you into the shower and suck your dick?"

Salt's eyes just about popped right out of their sockets as lust fired up bright and hot in his veins. "No, nothing else." He had questions about Andy's past, but he'd ask them later, or another time, maybe. He wasn't sure what the rules really were, what the boundaries were between them. For now, he'd settle for the offer of ecstasy in Andy's wicked grin. "You gonna take my boots off for me again?"

"Naked or dressed?" Andy asked, touching the waistband of his underwear.

"Like you really need me to answer that?" Salt leered just a little, hoping he didn't look like a total fool.

Andy's sweet laughter rang out. *Sweet? No, no, no. Don't go there. He's not mine to keep, and we don't know each other very well anyway.*

"Let me just shuck my underwear then. You do know you never put your shirt back on, right?"

Salt tipped his nose up haughtily. "I was trying to make sure you didn't want me to leave."

"I didn't, you know," Andy said quietly. "I really didn't. It freaked me out."

"Well, don't be freaked out. I'm a stud, and you can't help yourself." Salt winked and pointed at Andy when he laughed again. "Now cut that out before you wound my pride."

"You're something else," Andy told him. Andy stood up and pulled his underwear off. He twirled them on one finger and moved his hips in such a way that his softened cock swung from side to side.

Salt was torn between laughing or sliding right out of his chair and crawling over to suck that swinging shaft. He settled for raising one booted foot up. "Come on, show me what you got."

By the time Andy had straddled each leg and pulled off Salt's boots and socks, Salt's cock was hard enough to be used as a hammer. He stood and let Andy divest him of his pants and briefs. It was strange, letting someone else strip him, but Salt decided he liked it, especially when Andy fisted his cock and licked the tip.

"Oh, yeah," Salt sighed. "Do that much more and I'm gonna come before we get in the shower."

"That's all right. Motel showers are notoriously tiny." Andy was already on his knees. He raised Salt's balls up and suckled on them.

Salt swayed on his feet, his knees going a little weak as Andy gently thumbed over his frenulum. "Andy," he rasped, settling his hands on Andy's shoulders.

Andy hummed inquisitively and kept lapping at his balls. Salt had to put a hand on the table to hold himself up, then he gave up even that and sat back in the chair. Andy kept right on his balls, kept touching his cock so perfectly.

Salt spread his legs. His ass was definitely sore, his hole making him wince as he wiggled. Andy hefted Salt's nuts up and licked behind them, moaning happily. Damn, but the man did like licking him. Worked out well since Salt was enjoying the hell out of being licked.

The prod of a fingertip at his anus brought a hunger to the surface that Salt wasn't really expecting. As tender as that area was, he wouldn't have thought it'd feel good being touched there again, but the burn was slight and Andy didn't just shove that digit up there. He merely teased around and around Salt's rim while sucking on his ball sac.

Salt ran a hand through Andy's hair. It was softer than Salt had expected, and cool to the touch. His other hand cupped Andy's neck, just wanting to touch him. Andy left off Salt's balls and licked up the length of his cock.

The feel of that wet, hot tongue dragging over his cockhead was incredible. Salt gasped and struggled to keep his eyes open. Andy looked up at him through thick black lashes. The pleasure he saw in Andy's eyes surprised Salt. It was obvious from that, along with the sounds Andy was making, that he was enjoying what he was doing, possibly as much as Salt was enjoying it.

When Andy sucked him in almost to the base, Salt's eyes crossed before he slammed his eyelids shut as he shouted. The tight constriction of Andy's throat muscles was too much. Salt bucked and Andy bobbed up and down before taking him in deep again.

The teasing pressure around his rim combined with having his dick buried in Andy's throat was a winning combination. Salt grunted as he came, his entire body flushing hot then cold, his extremities tingling as he shot his load into Andy's mouth.

He could become addicted to having blow jobs like that, Salt decided a few minutes later when he could think again. Andy kept nuzzling his balls once Salt had to ask him to leave off licking his cock. Andy seemed content to stay down there licking at him. Salt opened his eyes and glanced down. He saw the white gobs of spunk on the carpet and figured Andy must have tugged himself off.

Showering was going to have to wait a few more minutes. Salt was too content to move, besides which, Andy seemed to be in some sort of lick-Salt-until-he-was-hard-again zone. Salt was game. It'd take a while, but it wasn't like he was going to rush out of the motel room again.

Chapter Eight

Parting wasn't a bad thing, Andy reassured himself as he opened the door to his apartment. Leaving Salt behind had nothing to do with the weird melancholy state he was in. If he was feeling more down than melancholy, well, that was merely a result of coming back to an empty place. Ever since Ty had moved out, the apartment seemed to scream with loneliness.

Andy scoffed at his fanciful thinking and shut the door behind him. He turned on the light and winced as the brightness assaulted his eyes. The living room was clean, something that still seemed wrong after the past year and a half. For the longest time there'd been messes all over. He used to bitch about them when he'd been tired and had to pick them up. Now he missed the chaos that, in memory, represented love and family.

"Shit, I'm just in a mood, aren't I?" His voice rang out in the empty apartment and Andy pressed his lips together. That was too pathetic for him to allow to happen again. The silence that followed his words only emphasised how very alone he was.

Andy sighed and shucked off his boots. He put them in the closet then settled his briefcase in there too. He'd deal with paperwork and sale orders later, after he'd showered and relaxed for a while.

There were no messages on his answering machine, no surprise. Hardly anyone ever called his landline nowadays. Andy wiped a layer of dust off the machine then turned on a few more lights as he walked through his apartment.

It was a spacious enough place, with three bedrooms and two baths. Probably too big for him now, but Andy had lived there for years and he liked the stability of staying there. Everything else might have changed, but this, at least, was still home.

Usually he plopped down and vegetated in front of the TV for a few hours after a week-long sales trip, but Andy found himself too restless to do so despite being tired. God, but he felt as worn as his favourite pair of jeans. Just as thin, too, like he was close to tearing in a few spots where he'd been rubbed more often than he could tolerate.

Scrubbing his hands over his face, Andy tried to push himself out of the strange funk he was in. It wasn't just coming home to such an empty place — he'd done that many times since Destry had passed away. Maybe he was going through a middle-aged crisis. Was thirty-seven considered middle-aged?

Andy considered it and thought that maybe it was. After all, the average lifespan for a man was around seventy-six years last he'd heard.

Now I'm depressing the hell out of myself. Who wanted to think that nearly half their life was gone and all they had to show for it was a start-up business and a big, empty apartment? And he knew full well that there were no guarantees anyone would live to be old. Destry sure hadn't.

Andy rubbed his temples, wishing he could rub the thoughts away. He closed his eyes and let himself think of the first thing that made him happy. Salt's lean, tough body appeared in his memory. The sound of Salt's deep, gruff voice rang in his ears. Andy's heart fluttered and for a moment he feared he was having some kind of heart attack.

When there was no pain and a sweet shimmer of arousal settled over him, Andy chuckled at himself. His morose thoughts on middle-age were making him paranoid. He wasn't so old that he didn't get horny thinking about the fantastic fuck he'd shared with Salt before leaving. And Salt? For an older man, he had incredible recovery time.

Warmth stole over Andy as blood rushed to his groin. His cock hardened and he forgot about being moody as he ran a hand down to cup his shaft through his jeans. As good as it felt to give himself a little squeeze, it was nothing compared to the way Salt had touched him.

Still, it was a hell of a lot better than worrying about how alone he was. Andy opened his pants right where he stood. He took his cock out and gave it a few strokes. That felt better, definitely. Not like someone else doing it, but not anything to bitch about, either.

Closing his eyes, he began a steady, rough stroke. Dry as his hand was, jerking off was kind of painful. He needed that to distract him from all the bullshit in his head, though.

Andy leaned against the wall and masturbated as he pictured Salt. The man's ass was tiny, tight, so perfect around Andy's dick. *What would it be like to come inside of Salt? To fuck him without a condom on?* Andy had never had that. How could he when he'd only had quick hook-ups and carelessness wasn't something he could afford?

But he tried to imagine it—the tight, hot, wet grip of Salt's ass around him. Those inner walls would ripple and work his length, would drive Andy out of his mind with bliss…

The dry, almost abusive way he was jerking off suddenly seemed an insult to the fantasy he was having. Andy gentled his grip and opened his eyes. He wasn't far from the bathroom, and he kept lube in there. Lotion, too.

It didn't take more than a few steps for him to have the lotion in hand. Andy pumped out a decent amount then rubbed his hands together, not wanting to give himself a shock from the coolness of the stuff. When he began stroking his cock again, he moaned and let himself fall right back into the streaming reel of him and Salt together, nothing between them but skin and lust.

He ached, a hollow core of need he didn't understand, but it wasn't stopping the welling of pleasure bearing up from his balls. Andy rolled his neck, biting his bottom lip as his nuts drew tight.

A loud, garish sound startled him just as he was picturing Salt's mouth gaping open, slack with impending orgasm. "Fuck!" Andy yelped, jerking his hand away from his cock as if he'd been busted in person instead of interrupted via phone.

With his hands slippery from the lotion, he couldn't take the phone out of his shirt pocket. The ring tone told him exactly who was calling—his brother Brandt.

"Talk about a cockblock." Andy grumbled some more as he wiped his hands off. His erection wilted enough for him to tuck it back in his briefs by the time he'd got the lotion off his palms. The phone had stopped ringing, too, but Andy knew his brother would just call back.

In fact, he was put straight through to voicemail when he tried Brandt's number. Andy hung up and waited the few seconds it took for Brandt to call him back.

"Do I even want to know what you were doing?" Brandt began with and Andy's normally calm nature gave way to his irritation.

"Get your damned mind out of the gutter, Brandt," he snapped. "And don't even try to tell me you weren't making some kind of dirty innuendo, because I know you and that tone you used."

Brandt huffed and Andy glared at the white wall across from him, seeing nothing but his own regrets. Too much time was spent wondering if he should have fought Brandt for Ty.

"You didn't email me anything or fax me orders—" Brandt began.

"I'm tired." *God, tired of so many things. Having my strings pulled like a puppet wielded by a spastic, sugar-snorting three-year-old.* "I've been gone all week, and just got home less than half an hour ago. I want food, a shower and a few hours of relaxing before tackling work again. Is that all right with you?"

Of course it wasn't, Andy thought as Brandt rattled on about how he needed everything right now. Andy knew better. Everything was taken care of, and Brandt could damn well check the orders online, but that wouldn't be as entertaining as fucking up Andy's evening.

When Brandt showed no signs of winding down, Andy was tempted to hang up. Ty's excited voice in the background, audible over Brandt's griping, was the only thing that kept Andy from disconnecting the call.

"Can I talk to him?" Andy finally asked when Ty kept pleading with Brandt for a few minutes on the phone with Andy. "Just let me talk to him for a bit then I'll get everything sent over to you."

It was always the same, with Andy caving because he wouldn't use Ty as a weapon against his brother. Brandt had no such compulsion, which was why he also had a majority interest in the company now than Andy did. Brandt controlled Ty's shares, which meant he controlled pretty much everything important to Andy — Ty included.

Instead of answering Andy, Brandt addressed Ty. "I don't know, Ty. Andy said he was really tired. He probably isn't up to talking to you."

"God damn it, Brandt," Andy seethed. "There's no call to hurt him!"

"You said you were tired," Brandt returned with. "Too tired to —"

Andy snapped. "You put him on the phone or so help me, I'll come over there —"

"Threatening me would be a very, very stupid thing to do," Brandt said in a low, angry voice. "You don't ever have to see Ty again, if that's the way you want to behave."

He didn't have to see Ty? All Andy wanted was to see him, to talk to him! Giving Ty up when Destry had died, well, it'd almost killed Andy, too.

Brandt knew it, and he'd delighted in sweeping Ty away. Andy had been too stupid with grief and too gullible to fight. He'd also thought Brandt really loved Ty and would offer him a stable home with family and —

Andy shook his head. It was done. He'd just given in without more than a token argument and the reasons why didn't matter. Brandt had told him Ty would never be allowed to stay with someone like him and Andy had believed it.

But he was tired of the threats. "I can sell feed for another company without being unemployed for more than an hour. We aren't the only ones pushing organic product now."

"You wouldn't," Brandt said. "You wouldn't trash Destry's dream."

He already had, by letting Ty go. "I'm done being pushed around."

"Uncle Andy has to go, but maybe he'll call you tomorrow," Brandt all but yelled right before hanging up.

Andy's eyes burned. So did his gut. He pressed a hand to his belly and tried to suppress a sob. He hoped to hell and back that Ty didn't believe Brandt, but considering how little Andy had got to talk to Ty in the past year and a half, he didn't know why Ty would doubt Brandt. Andy had been made out to be an uncaring, selfish bastard.

Brandt had always been so jealous of Destry and Andy's brotherly bond. Brandt was the youngest, though he'd only been two years younger than Andy. He'd never followed his brothers around, though. Brandt had always seemed to tolerate them even as he'd resented them. Destry and Andy had been close for several reasons, not the least of which was the fact that Destry was bi and Andy was gay. Brandt hadn't held back his disdain of either of those facts.

Yet... They'd let their younger brother in on the plans to build a company, and let him invest. Given him shares they shouldn't have. Andy had honestly thought, once Destry was diagnosed with cancer, that Brandt had truly had a change of heart. He'd been nicer, and seemed concerned for Destry.

Stop. Stop thinking about it. Andy looked at the phone in his hand. He yearned for someone to talk to about all the bullshit and stupidity in his life, but the only person who came to mind was Salt. Surely Salt wouldn't want to hear about his drama. They'd had great sex, and they'd conversed about general things, nothing too deep and meaningful. But it'd been nice. More friendly conversation than Andy had had with anyone else since Destry died.

More flirting and just plain fun, too.

Andy couldn't remember yearning so badly to speak to someone he'd had sex with before. Even as he ached to talk to Ty, to see his nephew and tell him the distance between them wasn't his doing, Andy also ached to talk to Salt.

Thumbing through his contacts, he found Salt's and stared at it. What would Salt think if he called? When they'd both agreed to keep it casual, no strings attached?

More than likely, he'd think Andy was a clingy weirdo. Andy snorted and started to exit his contact list. For some odd reason, he must have accidentally brushed the text feature.

"Well, a text, that's not as creepy, is it?" Then again, talking to himself was supposed to mean he was crazy. Andy didn't care. He talked out his problems more often than not. It was an easier way to untangle his thoughts.

"I could just let him know I'm home." *No, that implies I owe him a check-in. Definitely too stalkerish.* "Screw it. What's he gonna do, dump me? We aren't together." But maybe they were friends, sort of. Friends texted each other just for the hell of it, right?

Before he could talk himself out of it, Andy sent a quick text to Salt asking him if he was going to watch the boxing event everyone had been going on about.

No, I don't like watching two men beating the shit out of each other. Like the lovers, not the fighters.

Andy grinned. Yeah, he could get onboard with watching porn over fighting any time. Even the occasional sappy romance was preferable to a boxing match, although nothing beat a good action flick.

Within minutes, he and Salt were chatting via text. While it didn't solve his problems, it did give him something else to concentrate besides his own misery. Later, when he'd taken care of everything and was in bed, he thought of Salt, and smiled as he drifted off to sleep.

Chapter Nine

It was amazing how much he missed sex after having a few rounds of it with Andy. Salt was torn between being amused and irked at himself. He'd gone with nothing but his hand to get off by for over a year on more than one occasion. It shouldn't have been so hard to do so again, but the way Andy had fucked him, and the companionship they'd shared when not having sex, was probably what was messing with his head.

That, and the daily texting they were doing. Strangely enough, none of it was sexual, either. It'd started when Andy had left, and for over two weeks now, they'd spent at least a few minutes every day sharing stories about little things, or just saying hi.

Maybe it was a bad thing that Salt looked forward to those texts more than anything else. He was beginning to suspect his heart was going to be in danger if he wasn't careful. Andy was witty and charming, and despite them having screwed each other's brains out, Andy wasn't all about the sex.

If he had been, why would he have texted Salt so casually in the first place? Salt had already told him there was no need for strings. He'd be there any time Andy came to town.

But he'd been harbouring a secret hope, he now realised. So secret, he hadn't even been aware of it. Every text he got from Andy fed that hope, and Salt would catch himself daydreaming about having a real relationship with Andy. Waking up with him on the mornings Andy wasn't on sales trips, spending the evenings talking and hanging out together. Sex, of course, there'd be plenty of that, too.

Salt had some trouble picturing it all, but being around Carlos, Will and Troy helped to show him what a healthy, loving relationship could be like.

"Are you thinking about him again?"

Salt barely kept from jolting upon hearing Rocky's question. He blinked and looked down at the barbed wire he'd been stringing. "Sneaking up on me while I'm fixing the fence is just mean, Rocky."

She snorted and poked him on the shoulder. "Please. I made as much racket as a herd of bulls, you were just too busy thinking about lover boy to notice it!"

Salt was sure his cheeks were going to catch fire from the strength of his blushing. Hopefully his tan-darkened skin disguised any pink trying to make its way through. "I was trying to figure out how much wire to unroll for the measurements I made, plus the length to —"

"Uh-huh, sure ya were. I've seen you staring off with a goofy look on your mug more than once lately, and I think it's sweet. If you ever tell anyone I said that, I'll hurt you."

Salt glanced over his shoulder at Rocky. "What kind of friend are you?" he asked, teasing her because it was fun.

Rocky smirked at him. "The best kind to have. I won't let you lose a finger or an eye because you're busy fantasising about fucking your stud instead of concentrating on stringing wire."

Her bluntness still shocked Salt. He should have been used to it by now, considering that Rocky was his best friend, and yet he wasn't able to keep from guffawing with embarrassment.

"You're so cute when you're all befuddled," Rocky crooned right before cackling like the evilest witch in the world.

"I'm always cute," Salt retorted as he stood up from where he'd been squatting. "Damn, my back..." He stretched and his lower back, had it been able to, would have whimpered with relief. "This growing old shit sucks."

"Beats the alternative, which is dying young." Rocky whistled loudly. Salt cringed. "Let's have Ramsey and Duke finish over here. Ramsey needs to learn how to do his damned job."

Salt turned and watched the two men approach on foot after they hopped out of the truck bed. "You made them ride in the back?"

"Why not?" Rocky asked, watching them as well. "Ramsey and his questions annoy the shit out of me. He's a nosy fucker and if he were asking questions about how to do his job, I'd answer, but no. He wants to know everyone's business. I've about had it with him."

Salt cocked his head as he considered the younger man. "I don't trust him. Just gives me a bad feeling in my gut, but he seems harmless, and besides, what could he do?" Salt was afraid he might resent Ramsey because the guy was young and sexy as sin. He didn't trust his judgement on the man.

Rocky scooched closer to him. "Well, he could be a homophobic bastard posing as a gay man so he could get in here and kill everybody. Or something."

Salt gawped at Rocky. "That's more paranoid than anything I ever thought!"

"Close your mouth and keep it down," Rocky murmured urgently. "I have some fucking awesome conspiracy theories I need to share with you sometime."

He chose to ignore that offer, instead keeping them on track with discussing Ramsey. "He's not a homophobe. I've seen him checking out every man here excluding myself. Heard some very, uh, indisputable sounds coming out of the room he shares with Baxter, too. Not every night, but enough to know they're getting off together."

Rocky jerked her gaze his way. "How'd I miss that?"

"If you didn't snore so loud it rattles the windows you mighta heard them," Salt informed her. "Anyway, he's gay, but my gut tells me not to trust him. Don't know why."

"Maybe I should talk to Carlos." Rocky went back to watching Ramsey and Duke.

"Not yet. I wouldn't want to be responsible for a good man losing his job, in case I'm just being a jackass." Salt nodded as the other two cowboys drew closer. "Hey, Duke, Ramsey. Rocky's going to put you two on fence repair while we handle some other jobs."

Duke nodded easily, but Ramsey frowned.

Salt didn't like that at all. "Is this something else you never had to do at your last job?"

"I did it once," Ramsey said with a defensive tone to his voice. "It was years ago, so I'll need a refresher."

"I can do that," Duke offered. He was a plain-looking, easy-going man who carried a little softness around his belly despite how hard he worked. "I don't mind showing Ramsey the ropes."

"Or the barbed wire," Ramsey joked cringe-worthily. Duke groaned.

"Keep cracking jokes like that and Duke's liable to leave you in a gully wearing a string of spiked metal." Salt at least tried to joke with Ramsey, but as always, there was some weird intensity to Ramsey's eyes that made Salt think the other man was processing every word he spoke for a mysterious reason.

Shrugging off such paranoia, Salt waved at the men. "Call me on the two-way if you need anything."

"Call Carlos," Rocky corrected. Salt glanced at her and she grinned. "We have to go to town to pick up a feed order that just came in."

"Both of you?" Ramsey asked doubtfully.

Rocky turned and looked at him. "You got your job to do, we got ours. There's no need for you to be poking about in what we're doing."

Ramsey turned away and Salt felt a frisson of unease, but he couldn't pinpoint any reason for him to suspect Ramsey was less than he claimed to be.

Except that he seems to know about ranch work in a third-party kinda way, like someone told him what he'd be doing instead of him actually ever having done it.

"You just want to go back to the diner," Salt teased Rocky a short while later. "You're the one having raunchy on-the-job fantasies."

Rocky started the truck up as she laughed. "Oh, now, there ain't nothing raunchy about them! I would never think about treating my lady with anything less than the utmost respect and gentleness."

Salt just about chuckled himself silly. It took him a couple of attempts at getting a good breath before he could speak while Rocky glowered at him. "Sorry, but you know, Ms Jen looks like a lady, all prim and proper, and it's been my experience with men, granted, that prissy and perfect hides a tiger in the sack. The tighter they're wound, the fiercer they come uncoiled for ya."

Rocky waggled her eyebrows. "Ohhhh, then I am so gonna work on encouraging her to take a walk on the wild side."

"You can't convert someone—" Salt stopped. Rocky knew it, and it wasn't like she was going to force herself on the pretty waitress.

"She might be curious," Rocky told him while she drove them down the bumpy dirt road towards the main house and road. "Lots of people are, especially when they start getting older and wonder what they've missed."

Salt tried not to look shocked at that. He knew people were curious, but was Rocky saying she was willing to be used? Salt had to ask. "You'd let her mess around with you and use you?"

Rocky shrugged, but Salt didn't miss the pinched look that settled over her profile. "Why not? I keep wanting to jump right into serious with every woman I date. Might as well try something different. You can't bitch at me about it, either. You told me all you ever had was casual sex. It's my turn to give it a shot."

"Didn't realise it was a tag-team event," Salt groused, but he let it go. Rocky was an adult and who knew, maybe a casual fling would be good for her.

Except when they got to the diner, Salt could tell by the longing in Rocky's gaze that she was already infatuated with the waitress, Jen. There were, he was certain, emotions involved on Rocky's part, at least. He'd better start preparing for the coming letdown and misery she was probably going to experience.

They grabbed a seat at a table in the back of the diner—one right by the people Jen was waiting on. Rocky shot her a timid look as they sat. Jen nodded and returned a polite smile that she probably used on all customers.

Salt didn't like the whole timid bit. Rocky wasn't like that—she was gregarious, loud and obnoxious but fun and good-hearted. "Just be yourself," he mumbled softly. "Otherwise she might think you tricked her later on, if…well, if you two, you know."

Jen glanced at him and Salt winced. He'd been pretty damn quiet and didn't think she could have heard him, but she *was* a mom and his own sure had had super-hearing abilities. It went with the whole eyes on the back of the head thing as far as he was concerned. Moms were about as omnipotent as a human being could be.

"I'll be right with you," Jen said before heading over to the counter. Salt watched her pluck up two menus before he spoke again.

"Maybe you need to relax a little," he suggested.

Rocky rolled her eyes. "Being myself ain't got me nothing but a string of broken hearts. I'm not risking that kind of pain again."

"You seem to have gotten over Shelly quick enough. Are you sure you loved her?" Salt thought a broken heart should take months to recover from, not that he was any expert. It still seemed a good idea to get

Rocky to thinking about the strength of her feelings for Shelly.

Rocky opened her mouth and closed it again before covering her eyes with her hands. "Oh, hell. Maybe not. I don't even miss her. Didn't bother me at all to talk to her and tell her she wasn't getting another dime from me last payday." She peeked at him from between her fingers. "Maybe I'm in love with the idea of being in love. That's bordering on too deep a thought for me, but it'd explain why all my ex-girlfriends don't seem such a loss to me now."

"Surely you're being modest. An intelligent person would be cognisant of their issues, and it seems like you are aware of yours."

Salt jerked his head around and saw Jen standing beside their table at the same time Rocky did. Rocky dropped her hands to the table top as her face flamed scarlet. "I—I—it wasn't—I didn't—"

Hell's bells, he'd never seen Rocky so flustered! Salt couldn't bear to see her stumbling over her own words. "Rocky was just being modest. She's a smart gal."

Jen and Rocky both looked at him. Salt held up both hands. "Oh, come on, now. When did gal become politically incorrect?"

Jen brought her pen to her bottom lip and nibbled on it for a second before responding. "I suppose it hasn't."

"He didn't say I was smart *for a* gal," Rocky said as she nodded.

Salt huffed and held out a hand for a menu. "I'm not stupid. My mama would have skinned me alive if I'd ever even had a misogynistic thought."

Jen's smile seemed a lot more genuine when she turned it on him. "Ah, your mama and I raised our sons the same way."

Salt almost reached back and rubbed his backside at that. He'd had a wooden spoon put to his butt more than once as a kid when he'd screwed up. Didn't seem like abuse to him, either. If his mama hadn't kept him in line, there was no telling what all kind of trouble he'd have got into.

"You both work at the Mossy Glenn?" Jen asked.

Salt decided Rocky could do the talking. Rocky glanced at him then at Jen. "Yes. Salt and I have been there since the first hires. It's a great place to work."

"I imagine it is," Jen agreed before tapping her lip with the pen a few more times. She seemed to be working up to something.

"Everyone's real friendly, and it ain't like there's wild parties going on," Rocky continued, speaking a little faster than normal. "The ranch is doing well, too. Carlos was able to hire a few new hands about a month ago."

Jen took the order pad out of her pocket and went to tapping that with the pen instead. "Oh, okay. So I suppose there's no need for even a part-time hand out there?"

Rocky gulped, her eyes going round. Salt decided to bail her out again. "Well, ma'am, that depends on the bosses and whoever's applying. Would that be you who is interested?"

Jen waved him off. "No, of course not. I'm not—" She darted an apologetic look towards Rocky, and Salt knew then she'd definitely heard him a few minutes ago. Rocky averted her eyes and turned away. "I'm not sure I'd fit in there, but I suspect my son might."

"You suspect?" Salt felt his eyebrows climbing up his forehead.

Jen glanced around and so did Salt. The people beside them had left at some point and they seemed to be relatively alone with her.

Jen still leaned close as she spoke. "Barney hasn't ever told me he's interested in anyone, not women or men, but I suspect... I suspect he's afraid to tell me. I might have went on about wanting grandchildren years back before..." She shrugged.

Salt canted his head at her. "Being gay don't mean there can't be children and grandchildren for you."

"I was ignorant." Jen tucked a strand of brown hair behind her ear. "I went on about him marrying the right girl and all that, without thinking about how he'd never so much as dated a girl before. He always followed around Fred's boy."

"Freddie Jr." Salt knew all about that kid. He'd been badly abused by his daddy, and it might have broken something in him. Either that or the kid had been a pyromaniac psycho long before he'd almost killed people a few months ago.

Jen tapped that order pad again. "Yes, him. This whole community let that boy down."

There was no arguing with that, at least not to Salt. Freddie Jr's abuse hadn't been a secret according to what Salt had heard.

"Anyway. I was just wondering if there was anything he could do there. He's working two part-time jobs as it is right now, but..." Jen blushed and scribbled something on that pad. "Times are really hard."

"They are," Salt agreed. Rocky murmured her assent as well. "Let me talk to Carlos, and I'll see what he says." He didn't think there was any room—

financially at least—for another ranch hand, but he could be wrong. Salt didn't have shit to do with the books, so for all he knew, the Mossy G could be dragging in the big money. Of course, how that would happen without them selling off any stock was beyond him.

"Thank you." Jen beamed at him.

Rocky cleared her throat. Jen looked at her. "If Barney is straight as an arrow, the Mossy Glenn probably won't appeal to him."

"Let me or Rocky talk to Carlos first." Salt held out a hand to Jen. "I'm Salt, by the way, and that's Rocky."

Rocky shook Jen's hand next and Salt bit back a grimace at the way Rocky let her palm linger against Jen's. Rocky surely was setting herself up for disappointment.

"Here's my cell number," Rocky offered, rattling off the numbers. "Give me until tomorrow evening to talk to the boss. Then you can call or text me. This way you don't have to give out your number to someone you don't know."

Jen quirked an eyebrow at her. "Like you just did?"

Rocky spluttered then muttered something about being able to take care of herself.

"I assure you, so can I."

Damn, Jen sounded a bit miffed. Salt was just starving.

"Any chance I can get a burger and fries along with a glass of tea?" he interjected in the hopes of preventing any bickering. It sure looked like Rocky was about to insert her foot into her mouth again.

"Of course you can. I'm sorry, I'm being a horrible waitress." That fake smile was back as Jen put the tip of her pen to the pad. "How do you want your burger?"

Twenty minutes later, Salt and Rocky were outside sweating under the sun's rays. "That was maybe the most uncomfortable lunch ever, Rocky."

Rocky groaned. "My God, I know! I just had to make it sound like I thought Jen was some fragile flower. Ugh."

"Apologising might help."

Rocky shook her head. "You don't get it. Every time I tried to speak to Jen and tell her I was sorry, my throat damn near closed up on me! I've never been so nervous around a woman I was interested in before." Rocky paused and pursed her lips. "Of course, I'm usually in bed with a woman within a couple of hours of meeting her, too. Jen's different."

Salt prayed for more patience. "She's straight, Rocky. You heard her in there when we thought she wanted a job at the ranch. You need to look elsewhere for someone to date."

The stubborn look on Rocky's face told him it was a lost cause. They didn't speak again until that evening after supper.

"I'm not mad at you," Rocky said as she pulled him aside. "I was just thinking about what you said, is all. I can't help but feel there's more to Jen than what you're seeing. And she didn't say she wasn't a lesbian, or bi. She said she wasn't sure she'd fit in. That's not a no."

Salt couldn't hold back a sigh. "It's not a yes, either, Rocky. Chances are she just wants a job for her son and she's not willing to jeopardise that by saying she's straight. Or he's straight, I don't even know at this point."

Rocky bobbed her head. "That's right, you don't, so let me deal with it. I appreciate you being concerned, but I'm a big gal. I won't blame you if Jen shatters my heart into a million pieces."

"Melodramatic much?" he asked as he winked at her.

Rocky made shooing motions with her hands. "Duh. Now go talk to your boyfriend and have dirty text sex. You should just call him, you know. I'm going to chat with Carlos."

"We don't text sex, or sext, or have phone sex at all," Salt grumbled. "We're friends, not just fuck buddies." And it felt so good to say so even if he wasn't sure Andy felt the same way.

"You have fun with that." Rocky patted his arm and left.

* * * *

Texas was hot, miserable, muggy and the plant life looked to be dying off due to the almost constant state of drought the place was in. Andy knew there were prettier parts of Texas, but the area South of San Antonio was in bad shape. As hot as it was, he'd bet the water would evaporate right out of his bottle if he uncapped it outside.

After a sweat-soaked day—Andy hadn't ever sweated like he had making his sales calls today— Andy cranked up the AC in his hotel room and contemplated supper. No way was he going outside again. Even if the hotel caught on fire, he'd probably be cooler standing in the flames.

His phone chimed with his favourite tone and the exhaustion that had been settling over him vanished. Salt was done working for the day, too, it seemed.

Andy took his cell out and set it on the small table by the window. He made himself wait until he'd taken off his boots, socks, shirt and pants before checking the message. Getting cooled off was a priority above all else, even the one thing that made his days joyful.

Once he was stripped down, Andy checked the message and grinned. Salt started off with a lead-in about the lunch from hell. "Of course I want to know what happened, goofball." Andy typed those exact words in. Less than a minute later, he frowned at the reply. Did he want to talk to Salt instead of text?

Would that be breaking some non-relationship rule? "Are there non-relationship rules?" There was probably some *Idiot's Guide* book for those.

There'd been things he'd like to have shared with Salt over the past weeks, but texting them had been too tedious. He had a great story to tell about the rancher he'd just called on, too. One involving tarantulas and Andy acting like a terrified child. Damn, but he hated spiders.

Instead of texting Salt back and telling him to go ahead and call, Andy dialled Salt's number himself. Salt had taken the first step towards changing things between them, and Andy was willing to match him.

"Hey, Salt, what's this about the lunch from hell?" Andy asked right off the bat, and any fears he had about the whole conversation being awkward were quickly erased as he and Salt settled in for an hour-long chat.

* * * *

Friday night, Andy decided to check out the biggest gay club in San Antonio. It was packed, the music was loud and there were men all over the place.

Younger men, mostly. Still, he could work with that. He was horny, and tired of being alone. There was also the fact that he'd talked on the phone with Salt for the past three nights and was feeling kind of off-kilter about that. It was almost as if they were in a relationship, the way Andy lit up inside when he heard Salt's voice or got a text from him.

But there were no promises between them, and Salt was supposed to be heading to Helena for some work-related thing. Andy had kind of zoned out over that because he knew Salt used to go there to get laid periodically, just as he'd done at any big city in Montana when he could. Chances were good he'd do the same thing in Helena this time.

That caused something suspiciously painful to come to life inside Andy. It was an ugly, jealous, possessive thing that snarled and gnashed its teeth at the very idea of anyone else touching Salt.

Andy wasn't having that. He had no claim over Salt, and vice versa. They were friends, buddies, and if Salt was amenable to it the next time Andy was nearby, they'd be lovers then, too. For Andy to turn around and change the rules, to think he had any rights to Salt, well, that was stupid and he knew it.

It still left him with a hollow ache he couldn't get rid of.

Getting laid would help, he was sure of it. That would teach his mind and remind his body that he didn't have anyone who belonged to him. His heart wasn't even in the equation. It wasn't, Andy kept telling himself. He was just in a moody funk again like he had been weeks ago when Brandt had been such a dick.

Andy never did get to talk to Ty, either.

That's enough being morose. Time to feel good, at least for a while.

Determined, Andy waded through the men clustered all over the place. He was groped, called 'Daddy' more than he'd ever have liked to be and propositioned a half dozen times before he reached the bar. Maybe tonight wouldn't be a total loss after all.

Andy just hoped he could keep from thinking about Salt if he ended up fucking someone else.

Chapter Ten

The last thing Salt expected early on a Saturday morning was a call from Andy, but that was what he got as he stepped out of the bathroom while he was towelling off his hair. Salt tossed the towel down and hurried over to his phone. He was glad he had his own hotel room, and Rocky had hers. His nudity wasn't going to offend anyone.

Jesus, I hope nothing's wrong. Don't know why else he'd be calling this early though. "Hey, Andy, what's up?" Salt's pulse sped up and he held his breath.

"Salt, I just…" Andy paused, then a loud, gusty exhale came across the line. "Man, I don't know. I was wondering, do you think I can come out and maybe hang with you next weekend?"

Salt frowned. "I thought you were supposed to go to Georgia? I mean, I don't mind of course." He stopped short of telling Andy he'd be happy to see him again, afraid his effusiveness might put Andy off.

"I was, but I think I'm going to move that up, head to Georgia tomorrow. I'm tired of travelling, and I need a break."

Andy sounded tired, and there was a tightness to his voice that Salt didn't think was from the call being wireless.

"You okay, Andy?"

Andy's sharp, barked laugh made Salt wince.

"I don't know what's going on," Andy said. "I think maybe we need to talk in person. Maybe...maybe there's more to be said between us."

A chill skittered down Salt's spine. Was he losing Andy already? "Did I fuck up by starting the phone calls?" He didn't want to lose Andy completely. They could text, or not even do that, if Andy would come see him sometime.

"No, you didn't. It's me."

Salt snorted.

"Not like that," Andy snapped, sounding irritated with Salt for the first time Salt could remember hearing. "I mean, I'm—fuck. I don't even know, man." There was another loud breath. "What are you doing tonight? Oh, God, I promised myself I wouldn't ask. Last night, did you...did you..."

Salt took the phone away from his ear and looked at it like it'd sprouted tentacles. When Andy kept on spluttering, Salt brought the phone back to rest it against his head. "Tonight I'm probably going to be reading up on this new tack company Carlos sent me to check out. In an hour or so, Rocky and I are going to check the business out, see if their stuff is as high-quality as we've been told. Somewhere there'll be breakfast and lunch, probably. Maybe pizza for supper. What's going on, Andy?"

"Last night?"

At first Salt thought Andy was asking him, but Andy started talking.

"I thought since you'd be out looking for a lay most likely—"

"I wasn't," Salt cut in with. "I talked to you, then I went to bed." His gut got a little queasy. "What are you trying to get around to? Just spit it out instead of torturing us both."

Andy only hesitated for a moment. "I thought you'd be going out, even though you didn't, and the idea of you letting someone else fuck you just pissed me off. I didn't like it. But I know that's bullshit, right? Because we aren't exclusive. We're friends, and we had sex weeks ago. So, no exclusive claims. I went out, telling myself that. I was—I don't know. Angry, jealous, horny. Stupid."

Salt didn't want to hear about Andy's night out. Andy was a good-looking man, with a dick that could make any size-queen happy. He hadn't thought of Andy fucking anyone else—on purpose. Salt didn't want to picture that. "I don't want to know the rest."

"But—"

"No!" Salt almost shouted it, but he managed some restraint. "What you do is your business, unless you're doing it with me, then it's my business, too."

"Are you jealous?"

Salt wasn't so much as jealous as he was hurt, which was fucking stupid. "No. I knew you'd probably be getting laid all over the place, handsome stud like you. I just don't want to hear about it."

"It hurt me to think of you with someone else."

Salt froze, barely daring to breathe. Andy waited for a moment, then continued.

"So I was wondering if we could talk in person, and maybe change our agreement. Sounds like I want to negotiate a contract or something, doesn't it? But I— there's something about you, and us together. I've never had this kind of a friendship before, and I think there could be more between us. A year ago that would have scared the shit out of me. Now it's not so terrifying."

"I'm amenable to talking about it all," Salt finally got past his numb lips. He was so stunned. He'd thought he was the only one becoming attached in an emotional manner. Hearing that Andy was, too, freed up Salt's heart and allowed the budding of the affection he'd ruthlessly stomped out until then. "I'd like to have that talk."

"Next weekend, then?"

"Whenever you want, Andy." Salt closed his eyes and smiled as warmth bloomed inside his chest. There was a sweet shimmer of happiness he hadn't felt before spreading through him.

"I'll be there Friday afternoon. Earlier, if I can swing it."

"Sounds good. I might have to work Saturday or Sunday."

"Can I help you?" Andy asked.

Salt's grin was so big it made his face hurt. "Yeah, of course you can. And Andy?"

"Yes?" Andy replied.

"You don't have to worry about me hooking up with anyone else." He only wanted one man, though he'd keep that to himself.

Andy's chuckle was music to Salt's ears. "Thanks, Salt. Same goes on my end. See you on Friday."

"Count on it." Salt disconnected the call and had to work not to let out a whoop of joy. He didn't know Andy well in some respects—Andy didn't talk about his family or his past really. Salt liked what he did know of Andy, though, and thought him to be a decent guy.

Someone Salt would like an actual relationship with, certainly. Salt gave up trying to keep it all inside. He whooped and laughed, delighted and excited by the turn in events. Friday couldn't get there soon enough.

* * * *

Andy didn't tell Brandt why he'd rearranged his travel plans. Brandt would find a way to fuck Andy over if he suspected Andy might be finding a bit of happiness somewhere.

"Overreacting much?" Andy asked himself as he turned onto the road leading to the Mossy Glenn. There was no reason for him to think Brandt would go so far to make him miserable... Except that Brandt had already ripped Andy's heart out by keeping Ty from him.

Andy pushed aside those thoughts. There was nothing he could do about it all now, and he wanted to focus on him and Salt. Andy was nervous, like they hadn't already had sex and established a friendship. What he wanted wouldn't be any different, really. Just entailed them being monogamous.

That would have sent Andy running for the hills once upon a time—something Brandt had used in his argument as to why Ty would be better off with him and his wife Mary. Add in Brandt and Mary's two kids, and it had sure seemed like Ty would be better off in a stable family.

Well, there was Andy's mistake. Brandt was about as stable as a case of nitroglycerin in a tornado.

And Andy was ready to move past being a slut to finding something more. He thought he could have that with Salt. Wanted it with Salt, and Salt seemed to be on the same page.

So Andy was excited, and nervous, and horny. The three sensations kept swapping around for dominance, and by the time he pulled up to park the truck by the bunkhouse, he had a thin sheen of sweat on his brow despite the AC blowing on his face. He knew Salt hadn't changed his mind—they'd spoken on the phone every day since Andy had his relationship breakthrough.

Salt wouldn't ditch him now, but Andy was kind of terrified he might screw the whole deal up. Hell, Salt hadn't had any long-term relationships either, so between the two of them, they might be doomed to failure.

"No. Fuck that." Andy wasn't a pathetic quitter. He shut the truck off and unbuckled his seat belt. As he got out of the truck, he saw Carlos and Will standing on the porch. "Hey. How's it going?"

Carlos nodded, but Will bounced then darted down the steps, chattering as he ran. "Salt told us he's expecting you, and I'm so happy he's found someone! He's a great guy, you know. All tall and thin and studly, and kind and—"

Andy held up one hand. "Whoa, hold off. You don't have to sell me on him. I already like him."

Will stopped in front of him. "Well, you're gonna love him and he's going to be your world."

"Will," Carlos growled.

But Andy was floored, because there was something in that prediction that rang true to him. Even more, he yearned for a connection that went deeper than the surface.

"What? It's true," Will said loudly. "Salt might have liked Drake—Whoops." Will's eyes were just huge as he slapped a hand over his mouth.

Andy knew who Drake was, remembered the short, sexy guy. *Salt had liked him? I'm about as different from Drake as can be while still having the same private bits.*

"They didn't date or anything," Will said from between his fingers. "Drake's seriously, *seriously* committed to his cop boyfriend, Ian. I think Salt was just lonely."

"Salt is right here and thinking you shouldn't be talking about him," Salt said, walking up from the closest barn. "Ass."

Andy's heart did a slow roll as he watched Salt take long, steady strides towards him. The man was embarrassed, no doubt, but Andy doubted most people would see it. It was in the way he wouldn't meet Andy's gaze, and the lines etched around the corners of his mouth.

"I am an ass. A complete ass." Will dropped his hands to his hips then glanced at Carlos before turning his head back to look at Salt. "Totally an ass. To make up for it, you get the entire weekend off. Shoo."

Salt stopped a few feet away. He narrowed his eyes at Will, then at Carlos.

Carlos tipped his chin towards Salt. "It's fine, Salt. Take off. Will should have kept his mouth shut."

Andy thought he was the only one—besides Carlos—who saw Will flip Carlos off behind his back.

Salt cleared his throat and Andy returned his attention to the cowboy. Will and Carlos might as well not have been there once Salt raised his gaze to Andy's.

"Think I'll do that," Salt rasped. Andy flushed with the heat of desire. His cock began to grow erect and he had enough sense to know he didn't want to put on a show for anyone other than Salt.

"Ride with me?" Andy asked, aching to embrace Salt but afraid it'd be the wrong thing to do. His hands twitched as he thought of touching all of the places that made Salt cry out for him.

"Be glad to. Let me just get some clothes together." But Salt didn't move and after a long moment, Andy looked around to see that Will and Carlos had left. With them gone, he was freer to speak.

"You won't be needing more than what you have on," Andy informed him in a low voice. "I plan to keep you naked until you have to come back here."

Salt shivered, a delightful sight to see. "Toothbrush. I need that and deodorant."

Andy hadn't thought to grab an extra toothbrush. "Okay, but the sooner we're in the room, the sooner I can strip you down and make you mine." He almost gasped at his own words. They weren't what he'd intended to say, but sometimes over-thinking was a mistake. The words felt true, too, so he didn't try to backpedal out of them.

Salt stared at him for a minute and Andy fought against shuffling his feet as he wondered if he'd gone too far, too fast.

Then Salt moved quick as a flash, coming forward and grabbing Andy by the shoulder. Andy quickly found himself in the very embrace he'd wished for. Almost, anyways. He wasn't sure where to put his arms, what to do with his hands or what to say, but when Salt pressed up against him, Andy's world was right for a short time.

"Sorry if this is too much," Salt whispered by Andy's ear. "It's just good to see you."

There was so much meaning in those words, and Andy didn't think he was imagining it. He had his arms around Salt, running his hands over the planes of his back, in a heartbeat. "Don't apologise. I wanted to do this but was too damn scared."

"You don't ever have to be scared with me, Andy." There was the faintest feathering of lips against his neck, then Salt pulled back and grinned at him. "Now, let me grab a few things. Come on over to the bunk house. Everyone's still out working. I stayed close after lunch because I couldn't make myself do anything else. Damned barns are as spotless as they can be."

Andy laughed, just happy to be there with Salt. He followed Salt to the bunkhouse and waited on the couch while Salt gathered whatever he was going to bring.

The woman Salt had been with at the feed store, Rocky, came in before Salt was done. She made a beeline right to Andy's side, plopping down beside him.

"Don't be a dick to him or I'll break you," she said succinctly.

Andy figured her biceps were at least as big as his. He wasn't a fool, most of the time. "I'm not going to promise *you* anything. What's going on between Salt and me, that's our business. I know you're concerned about him, but Salt is a grown man and for all you know, he might end up breaking me."

Rocky looked shocked, then angry as she opened her mouth to reply, but the sound of Salt's boot heels striking the floor shut them both up.

Rocky hopped up and strolled over to Salt. "Hey, guess what? Carlos said he'd consider hiring Barney part-time. Only took Carlos weeks to finally tell me that. Jen was ecstatic."

Salt didn't appear to be thrilled. "And what does Barney think about it? His mama doesn't even know if he's gay. Barney might not want to be working here."

Rocky smacked him on the chest, not too hard, but it wasn't a pat, either. "Don't be silly, dude. His mama knows him. If Jen says he's gay, then he is. She's going to try talking to him about how she maybe accidentally encouraged him to hide that from her."

Salt's frown showed just how unhappy he was about Rocky's statements. "First off, mamas can be wrong. Mine was. She thought for sure I was straight and going to go into the priesthood. Go figure that one out. Second, you been talking to Jen a lot?"

Rocky didn't answer, instead heading for the door. "Have fun, you two."

"Is she mad?" Andy asked, confused by the interaction.

Salt shook his head. "Nah, she just doesn't want to talk about her crush on Jen."

"That's the waitress you told me about, right?" Andy remembered the conversation, but he wanted to be sure.

"Yeah, that's her. Jen seems real nice, and real straight, but I wonder if I'm reading her wrong and she isn't so nice. I don't really know her." Salt set down a small duffle then took off his cowboy hat and ran the fingers of one hand through his hair. "I just worry about Rocky. She's been hurt a lot."

"She worries about you, too," Andy said. "It's nice that you have someone here looking out for you."

Salt put his hat back on and sighed. "Okay, what'd she tell you?"

Andy picked up Salt's bag. "Only that she would break me if I was a dick to you. Figured telling her I'd be giving you dick was too cheesy."

"Too cheesy for her, but you didn't have a problem sharing it with me." Salt chuckled and shook his head. "Damn, that's bad, man."

Andy was glad Salt was past his embarrassment from earlier, and seemed to be in a good mood. He found himself doing something he'd never done with another male, except for Ty, and Destry when he'd been dying. Andy caught Salt's hand with his free one and held it. The dry, warm, callused skin sent a shiver over Andy. *God, how is it I've missed him when we've been talking and texting all the time?*

But he had, there was no denying it. Andy set the bag down again and turned to Salt.

"What—" Salt began, but Andy cupped his jaw and kissed Salt. The way Salt's lips pressed against his, the feel of his slick tongue rubbing alongside of Andy's, was pure magic. Andy gripped Salt's ass with his other hand, pulling Salt up to him so they were pressed together as closely as possible in their current state.

Salt moaned into the kiss and scraped his teeth over Andy's bottom lip. Andy growled as Salt held onto him, clinging with strong arms around Andy's torso.

Never had Andy experienced anything like the need thrumming through him. There'd been the thrill of landing a new guy before, that excitement at learning a body and wondering if there'd be something special about the person, something that would explain people's need to connect and form a couple.

He'd never figured that last one out, until Salt. Andy knew his body, knew the sounds and sighs, the way Salt moved for him, how he looked when he came. Knowing that didn't dim anything—it merely fed Andy's anticipation to experience it all again and again. There was something about the man in his arms that called out to Andy, and he was too tired of being alone to let his fear of commitment take the lead anymore.

So he held Salt tighter and kissed him with a possessive fierceness that left them both hard and shaking. When Andy raised his lips from Salt's, and opened his eyes, Salt's stunned expression was the first thing he saw. Stunned, and so turned on it looked like he ached with need. Salt's lips were swollen and red, wet and tempting.

Andy had to suck on them, taste the man once more. Salt grunted and slid his hands down to Andy's butt. He pulled their hips together and began to rut against Andy.

As good as that felt, Andy didn't want to put on a show for any of Salt's co-workers. He ended the sensual assault on Salt's mouth by moving back slowly. "I want you, but not here, where anyone can see us."

Salt nodded jerkily. He touched his lips, his eyes on Andy's. "Never been kissed like that. Like I'm important."

Why that broke Andy's heart, he didn't know. He'd never kissed anyone like they truly mattered, either. What a pair they were. "You are."

Those two words brought a pleased expression to Salt's face. He bent and picked up his hat which had fallen off at some point. Once he had it on, Andy grabbed his duffle and took Salt's hand in his free one.

They left the bunkhouse and were immediately greeted by whoops and whistles when they stepped out onto the porch. Several ranch hands stood in the yard razzing them. Andy took a little bow and Salt just laughed.

"Get back to work, you nosy scoundrels." Salt shook his head. "You can't tell me everything's done."

One cowboy came up onto the porch steps. He had pale blue eyes and dirty blond hair. A thin scar bisected his right cheek from the ear to the corner of his mouth. "You taking off for the weekend?"

Salt drew up short and frowned at the man. "Yeah, Ramsey, I am."

The cowboy, Ramsey, looked Andy over in a not-so-subtle way. Andy wondered if Salt had any idea the man wanted him. Salt hadn't mentioned Ramsey except to say he didn't trust the guy, and felt bad as he had no justification for his feelings. Andy thought maybe Salt was confusing signals and that Ramsey's interest was putting him on edge.

Andy gave Ramsey a smile that was all teeth. Ramsey narrowed his eyes but gave the barest nod before stepping back. "Y'all have fun."

"Okay?" Salt's confusion echoed in that solitary word, but neither Ramsey nor Andy explained the why of that. Andy waited until Ramsey was out of the way, then he and Salt went down the steps. A few more people teased them, but they just laughed it all off.

Chapter Eleven

When they were in the truck and on the road to Ashville, Andy finally brought up Ramsey. "You didn't tell me he had a scar. Or that he likes you."

Salt snapped his head around so fast that he smacked the passenger window. "Ow. Fuck. What are you talking about? He don't like me. As to the scar, I just don't see it, I guess. I mean, I noticed it when I saw him the first time, but no one wearing a scar wants to be gawked at, so I just ignored it. Figured if he ever wanted to explain it he would. Didn't matter to me. And he don't like me."

Andy figured he must be wearing a goofy grin. Salt was so sweet and naïve despite his age. "He does too. Didn't you see him sizing me up? He wasn't a happy man at all."

"He's just a nosy bastard," Salt muttered. "Always asking questions. I think he lied about his job experience. There's too much he doesn't know 'bout working on a ranch to have been a hand for three years."

Andy considered that for a moment. "Maybe, or maybe whatever happened that left the scar on him messed up his brain. Could have caused memory loss or something."

"I hadn't thought of that." Salt sighed and groaned. "Well now I feel like a total asshole."

"Don't," Andy said firmly. "He's eyeing you like he wants to fuck you and I have no sympathy for him for that reason alone."

Salt snorted and shook his head. "Nah, man, he doesn't look at me like that. You must have read him wrong."

Andy hadn't, but arguing was pointless. The fact that Salt didn't even notice Ramsey's desire, that he refused to acknowledge it, only proved that Salt was uninterested in the man. "I didn't, trust me on that, but I'm glad you don't return his interest."

"I don't. For one, he's too young. Second, he just seems sneaky to me."

Andy still thought that was likely because the man had been ogling Salt all along, but he didn't say so. "Too young? He's what, maybe thirty?" Ramsey had an unlined complexion — something which, considering his job, did seem odd.

"Twenty-seven, according to his application. Carlos showed it to me when he was considering hiring him." Salt put a hand on Andy's thigh. "Let's forget about him. I'd rather think of all the things we're gonna be doing to each other this weekend."

Andy grinned. "Yeah, me too, but there's that talk we need to have first."

Salt gave his thigh a squeeze. "Well then, why not have that talk now so you can fuck me into oblivion as soon as we get to the room?"

Andy pretended to be aghast. "Why, Salt, do you only want me for my body?"

Salt snickered. "No, but it doesn't make me want you any less, either."

Salt made him happy. The man was under his skin and Andy liked it. He licked his lips and tried to organise what he wanted to say, but decided he was over-thinking it all. He just needed to tell Salt how he felt.

"We don't have to talk," Salt said, breaking into Andy's thoughts. Andy glanced at him for a second before focusing visually on the road again. "Talking can be hard. Finding the words, explaining what you feel and being afraid to screw that up. You don't want to say the wrong thing and risk getting hurt, or scaring off the person you're talking to. So it's okay if you want to skip getting too deep. We could just agree to seeing each other only, if that's what you want, and leave it there."

"You're a braver man than me," Andy told Salt. "I get all the words bottled up. Bad thing for a salesman, I know, but it only happens when something important and personal is coming up. I can talk about feed all day long, yet when it comes to the things and people that mean the most to me, I can't explain—" Andy stopped, appalled at how much he had shared.

"It's okay, Andy. Telling me that doesn't make you a weak person." Salt ran his hand up from Andy's thigh to his shoulder. "As men, we're taught from early on to be strong and silent when it comes to our feelings. Kinda stupid, I think. Holding everything inside can't be healthy, either physically or mentally."

"It isn't," Andy murmured. "I don't like arguing. I'm not good at fighting for anything, I guess. For anyone. If I was, I'd never have let Ty go."

* * * *

Unexpected pain shot through Salt's chest. There was a load of hurt in Andy's voice. Salt tried not to let his leak through in his words. "Ty? You've never mentioned him. Was he—" Salt stopped himself from saying, 'someone you loved', because obviously, Andy had loved him. Still loved him, if Salt was any judge of the man's expression.

"He's my nephew," Andy said in a broken voice. "Destry's son. I helped Destry raise him when Ty's mama handed him over after giving birth to him. Destry and I shared an apartment for financial reasons, and because we were close. Brandt always seemed to be jealous of our relationship, yet when we tried to include him, he wouldn't have anything to do with us."

Salt's gut clenched as he listened to Andy talk. They were almost to town, but Andy had slowed the truck down as he spoke. "When Destry got sick, we thought it was just another bug he'd picked up. Destry was always catching anything that was going around. We didn't expect for the doctor to diagnose him with pancreatic cancer. Shit, Des was only thirty-eight."

"I'm sorry for your loss." Salt was—so very sorry. He wanted to hold Andy and let the man cry out some of the pain he was holding in.

"Thank you." Andy licked his lips then continued. "Des wanted me to raise Ty, but Brandt started acting like a decent person when we told him about the cancer. Started spending lots of time around Des, Ty and me. I think now that was because of the company. Des really went after getting it started. He wanted to leave Ty something, a legacy and a way to support himself. When Brandt asked to invest, after a year of acting like a decent guy, Des and I thought it was a sign of things improving. Brandt changing." Andy snorted.

"Man, was I a fucking idiot. Destry passed away with me and Ty holding his hands. Brandt showed up an hour later and pulled me aside as his wife Mary comforted Ty."

"Brandt talked you out of keeping custody of Ty?" Salt guessed.

"Yeah," Andy said with a small nod. "He pointed out that he'd become a better person, and he regretted the lost time with Destry. Ty seemed to get along with Brandt, and Brandt has kids with Mary. Younger than Ty, but still, they're old enough to be company. Brandt pointed out that he could give Ty a family, whereas all I could give him was an uncle who catted around when he got the chance."

Andy turned into the Super 8 parking lot. "I put up a token argument, but it seemed like everything I could come up with, Brandt shot down. When Mary came in and told me Ty wanted to go home with them, I figured..."

"Did she mean for the night?" Salt asked. If he ever met Brandt, he was likely going to jail for assault.

"I thought she meant to live," Andy admitted. "I think now that's what they wanted me to think. I think they planned it all out, every bit, so they could control Ty's shares of the company as well as Brandt's. Basically he's my boss now, which is bullshit considering he didn't come into the business until Des was diagnosed. So, you see what a fucking idiot I was? I am? I gave up the one person alive I still loved with everything in me."

"You can't get him back? Did you sign over custody?" Salt unsnapped his belt buckle as Andy parked.

Andy sighed and rubbed his eyes. "I did. They kept telling me Ty didn't want to see me, he wouldn't take my calls. Told me he hated me. It was true, to a point. I finally managed to speak to Ty by waiting outside his school one day. Ty was angry. Thought I'd just given him away because he was too much trouble. I tried to clear that up with him, but I don't know that he ever believed me."

"Do you get to talk to him now? Ever see him?"

Andy shrugged. "Brandt likes his control. When I do see Ty, or talk to him on the phone, Brandt is right there making sure neither of us can really talk."

Salt really didn't like Brandt at all. Or Mary, for that matter. "What about Internet? E-mail and all that?"

"Brandt doesn't allow the kids on it." Andy unbuckled and gave himself a shake. "Anyway, it's all my fault for not fighting for Ty, and not talking to him myself."

"They hit you up immediately after the death of your brother," Salt pointed out. "Manipulating you and Ty both at the worst moment in your lives." Salt thought of something else. "What about Ty's mama?"

"Dead," Andy bluntly informed him. "Heroin."

"Oh." There wasn't much to say about that. Salt got out of the truck, taking his bag with him.

Andy joined him as they walked to the room. "I don't want to spend this weekend thinking about all the mistakes I've made. I just want to be with you. I've...I've never felt like this about another person before. Never wanted anything serious."

"I've wanted it, I think, just never thought it'd happen." Salt waited until Andy opened the door and they entered the room. "I want you to know, I mean it when I tell you I'll be monogamous. I want something substantial, long-lasting with you."

"I want that, too." Andy framed Salt's face with both hands and stared into his eyes. Salt's heart was fluttering like mad in his chest. "I want you. I want to feel you without anything between us. I won't screw around on you, either. I've sowed my wild oats and don't have an interest in doing so again."

Salt loved hearing all of that, but his mind went to one part in particular. "Nothing between us? You mean without…" He gulped as want doubled inside him. "Without condoms?"

"Oh, God," Andy groaned, eyes nearly closing. "So much, yeah I want that. Never went bare with anyone else before. I want to feel you when I'm fucking you, feel everything…"

Salt began to tremble as he envisioned it. His hands shook wildly as he stepped away from Andy.

"We don't have to—" Andy began, but Salt held up one hand to cease the flow of words.

"I brought this, because I was going to broach the subject, too." Salt took out his wallet. Inside was a slip of paper he'd wanted to show Andy. He unfolded the letter from the lab. "I had this done again. Knew I was okay, because I'd been tested when I got the health insurance months back." Andy took the paper. "I hadn't been with anyone else since the insurance test, so I knew it was okay, but thought you might feel better seeing this."

Andy was smiling like he was on the verge of giggling or something. He handed the paper back to Salt. "I'd have trusted you, Salt. All the talking we've done, I've come to know you, and that's why I'm here now, wanting more than just sex." Andy winked at him then and took out his own wallet. "It's also why I went and got tested again, too."

Salt snickered as he took the paper. "What a pair we are. All the talking we've done, maybe we should have talked about some of these things — relationships, commitment. Or maybe not. I like that we did it in person."

"Me too." Andy took the paper back and tucked it away. "Now, I gotta tell you, Salt. I want you so bad I won't last more than a few minutes."

Salt knew the feeling. His dick was working its way to fully erect, but as horny as he was for Andy, he'd be going off like a bottle rocket with a short fuse. "Same goes. Let's get naked then get to round one. Next time you can fuck my ass until I can't walk, but right now, I want to suck you until you melt."

Andy wrinkled his nose at Salt. "Melt?"

Salt rolled his eyes. "Aw, hush up. I'm just an old cowboy who don't have all the fancy words to charm you."

"You charm me fine and dandy, stud." Andy took Salt's hat off and set it on the table. "You can make me melt, too. That mouth of yours is plumb magic."

Salt reached for Andy's shirt at the same time Andy reached for his. They smacked hands together and laughed. "You do yours, I'll do mine. Whoever gets naked first gets to pick the position we do this in."

"A competition — I like it," Andy purred. Salt grinned and reached for his own shirt. Andy leered at him then grabbed the collar of his own shirt and ripped, sending buttons flying.

"That's cheating!" Salt proclaimed, trying to get his buttons undone.

"Nope, no other rules were laid out." Andy whipped the shirt off then started on his boots.

Salt got his shirt off a moment later. No matter how fast he tried to be, Andy still got naked first, then Salt had to stop what he was doing and stare at all the perfect male flesh before him.

Andy's legs were paler than his upper body, and they were sheened in a layer of fine brown hair. His balls hung low between well-muscled thighs, and his cock stood tall and proud, the tip already beaded with pre-cum.

Andy's tiny waist offset his broad chest and shoulders. His nipples were bigger than Salt's, a coral colour and framed with whirls of dark hair. The nubs protruded, hard and begging for attention.

Salt kicked his jeans and underwear off, the last of his clothes he needed to shed. Like a man in a daze, he moved over to Andy, staring at his tits. Andy raised his arms up, baring his hairy pits. He put his hands behind his head and cocked his chin. "Come and get 'em."

Salt didn't need to be told twice. He pinched one nipple and dragged his teeth over the other. Andy's skin had a spicy taste to it that made his mouth water. Salt went after the nipple in his mouth, tonguing and suckling it as Andy began to pant.

Andy's cock was hot and hard between them, pressing alongside of Salt's. Salt pushed his free hand between them so he could feel that rigid shaft.

"Oh fuck," Andy rasped, gripping his shoulders tightly. "Salt, you're gonna make me come just from this, and I'm supposed to get to..."

Salt would let him choose the position in a minute. He was too busy sucking Andy's nipples, moving back and forth between them, to speak up just now though.

Andy slid his hands down to grasp Salt's ass. He wasn't gentle as he wedged his fingers between Salt's cheeks. A dry finger teased his hole and the instant that Salt gave a hard tug to Andy's nipples, that digit sank into his hole.

Salt threw his head back on a moan as his eyes crossed. Andy went after his neck, biting and marking him, as if claiming Salt's skin.

The finger in his ass was driving him insane, just missing his gland. Salt knew if he could arch just so, he'd get that deep touch he was craving. "Please, please, please," he got out, trying to shove back to get a deeper penetration.

Then Andy was sliding down, licking, biting his way to Salt's dick. Salt swayed and Andy stood up again. "Can't have you falling over on me."

Salt started to take a step back, but Andy growled and grabbed his hip. He pumped that finger in and out of Salt's asshole a few times then pushed it in as far as it'd go. "Let's see if we can do this."

'Do what,' Salt wanted to ask, but he'd lost the ability to speak as Andy began moving them towards the bed, that digit still inside Salt. Every step brought contact to his inner walls and made him clench with need.

Andy kept kissing him, too. His lips, his jaw, his neck—everywhere the man could reach was blessed by those firm lips. Salt was going to lose his ever-lovin' mind from all the attention being showered on him.

When his left calf whacked the bed frame, Salt almost yelped with relief. He was close to collapsing as his joints went weak from pleasure. Andy laid him down, taking that torturous finger from his ass before doing so. Salt regretted its loss, but Andy lapping at his cock head made him forget about everything else.

"So sexy," he thought he heard Andy say, but with his pulse racing, his heartbeat pounding in his ears, Salt couldn't be sure. He canted his hips as Andy suckled his crown, licking at that mind-altering spot on the underside of it. Salt grabbed at the blankets on the bed, trying to keep from shouting the place down. He hitched his legs up, heels set on the mattress.

Andy took advantage just as Salt had meant for him to, sliding spit-slicked fingers into his ass.

"Yes," Salt hissed, closing his eyes and trying to ride those digits. "Yes, fuck yes—"

Andy thrust in hard and fast, but he brushed over Salt's gland and set his inner nerve endings to dancing with pleasure. Salt rolled his head as he writhed. His hole ached as he was stretched, but the delicious pain twined in a perfect dance with the blissful sensation of Andy sucking his dick down to the base.

Slick, wet heat and constricting muscles massaged Salt's shaft. Andy bobbed up again then back down. He rubbed his nose against Salt's pubes and worked his tongue all over Salt's length.

There'd never been a blow job like the one he was getting, at least not for him. Andy reached up and tweaked Salt's nipple at the same time he lapped over Salt's slit. It was too much, when combined with the fullness in his ass.

Salt jolted as ecstasy streaked up from his ass to his spine. The sound he made was unearthly as it was torn from him, his cock pulsing cum into Andy's mouth as those wily fingers stroked Salt's prostate.

Moaning continuously, Salt could only shake and come in what seemed like an endless stream of release. Eventually he came back to reality, the bliss ebbing only to spike up in a different way as Andy crawled up his body.

"Open up," Andy commanded, gripping Salt by the hair atop his head. Salt's poor, tired dick tried to come to life again at the commanding tone Andy used, but it was simply too soon.

Andy shoved a pillow under his head, then another one. Salt parted his lips after licking them, and Andy grunted as he pushed his thick cock past them. Salt sealed his lips around Andy's shaft and sucked as he tongued the length of it.

He looked up and locked gazes with Andy. The intensity in Andy's expression was sexier than anything Salt had ever seen. Andy was burning for him, losing control as he thrust deep and breached Salt's throat.

Salt wasn't quite prepared for that, and he gagged as he reached up to cup Andy's ass.

"Sorry," Andy whispered as he started pulling back. Salt clutched Andy's ass hard enough to leave marks, tugging him forward. Andy resisted, then he gave in with a groan, his lashes fluttering down as his breath stuttered.

Andy's butt went rock hard beneath Salt's hands. His cock swelled in Salt's mouth, then Andy snapped his eyes open and he pulled his cock free of Salt's mouth. Salt started to protest, but Andy fisted his length and shouted as he pumped the first jet of cum onto Salt's face.

Oh hell, that's hot. Each spurt of spunk made Salt crave the next. He caught some on his tongue and lips. The salty, bitter taste was exquisite. Salt peeked up through narrowly slitted eyes and took in the state of Andy in orgasm.

Stunning, there was no other word for it. Andy's expression proclaimed his rapturous experience. The tendons in his neck stood out and his lips were parted, his eyes closed more often than not as he tried to coat Salt in his cum.

There was something primal about it, as if he were being claimed, marked, covered in Andy's scent. Salt was torn between rubbing it into his skin, or scooping it all off and swallowing it.

As Andy whimpered and collapsed beside him, breathing heavily and reaching for his arm, Salt settled on a compromise, rubbing some in then licking his fingers clean.

"God damn, that's something to see," Andy said in a gritty voice a moment later. "Holy fuck." He propped up on one arm and used his other hand to touch a spot beneath Salt's eye. Gently, Andy rubbed, then he held his finger to Salt's lips. "Suck."

Salt did, enjoying it all the more because Andy told him to do it. Andy's eyes went nearly black as his pupils expanded. "I'm going to fuck you raw."

"You better," Salt got out. "Just as soon as you're able."

Andy snorted and kissed him so fiercely Salt tasted blood. His or Andy's, he didn't know and it didn't matter. It was another mixing of their fluids. As romantic and silly as it might have sounded, to Salt it was a binding, a promise.

When Andy raised his head up, he was smirking. "You make it sound like that's gonna take a while, but let me tell you, with a stud like you waiting for it, my dick has an amazing recovery time."

Andy wiggled and sure enough, his cock was more hard than not against Salt's hip. "I think I should get to pick the position again."

Salt gulped, suddenly nervous, though he didn't see how he could screw up getting fucked. He realised it was because of the nature of the act they were going to share, with no barriers between them.

"I want to see you," Andy told him, caressing his cheek, turning those big eyes on him. "I want to see your eyes as I push into you. Make you mine."

"This is big," Salt got out past his too-tight throat. "I told you, never did anything like this before, and it means..." He had to swallow twice before he could continue. "It means something to me. More than us just agreeing not to fuck around. More than that."

Andy kissed him so tenderly then that Salt's eyes burned with tears. He wasn't ashamed — sometimes cowboys *did* cry despite the saying proclaiming otherwise.

"I want to love you, Saul Johnson," Andy said quietly, staring into his eyes. "I think I can love you, if you'll have me. You will, won't you?"

Salt thought maybe he was already a little in love with Andy. Saying so when he was feeling rather emotional wasn't something he wanted to do. But he could be honest. "I want you to, and yeah, I'll have you if you'll put up with this old cowboy."

"Sexy cowboy," Andy told him. "None of that old shit. You aren't much older than me."

"I look a lot older," Salt pointed out. "Got all these lines and wrinkles."

"You're a sexy fucker and you know it." Andy bent and nipped his cheek. "Stop being modest. You have got to know how much you turn me on." Andy rocked that hard cock against him again. "And you know what? As much as I want to be inside of you, I think maybe we should take a step back, let the anticipation build while we have pizza and watch stupid TV shows. What do you say? I have an ice chest full of your favourite beer."

Salt knew it wasn't a rejection. They'd both be hotter for it after waiting a few hours, and yeah, he wanted it to be as memorable as Andy did. "I'm good with that. I get to shower, too." Salt waggled his eyebrows. "Get everything nice and clean for you."

Andy's eager look, the way he licked his lips as he dragged his gaze down Salt's body, had Salt on the verge of begging for Andy to fuck him after all, but Salt found some restraint.

"Shower, and I'll order the pizza. If I get in with you, there won't be any waiting," Andy said, getting off the bed. He fisted his cock and gave it a stroke. "Once I get this inside of you, I don't plan on it coming out all night." He winked at Salt. "That's what getting off quick the first time does to me."

Salt could hardly wait.

Chapter Twelve

Andy couldn't explain all the reasons he wanted to wait a little while before laying Salt out on the bed and losing himself in the man. Part of it was because he'd just come—and damn, he'd needed to get off. He would have lasted maybe three strokes if he'd barebacked Salt's ass right off the bat.

Salt's tight little ass flexed beautifully as the man walked to the bathroom. Andy still had his cock in hand as he watched Salt. When he paused at the bathroom door and peered over his shoulder at Andy, Andy almost went after him.

"Go on. I'll take care of getting us some food."

Salt beamed at him then entered the bathroom. He didn't shut the door.

Andy knew with a sudden insight part of the reason he didn't want to toss Salt back on the bed and fuck him like a beast. Sappy, that was what he was, because he wanted to take his time and make love to Salt. It was about so much more than just getting off, what was going on between them.

For someone who had thought he'd never want to settle down, Andy was finding himself more than willing to—with Salt. To be fair, he might have considered giving a relationship a shot years ago, before he'd moved in with Destry.

When he'd said Destry tended to get sick easy, that'd been an understatement. Somewhere along the way, Des had been exposed to something that had compromised his immune system. Doctors could never pin it down, but Des had sworn it was from well water he'd used one summer on a friend's farm right before Ty was born.

Pancreatic cancer wasn't the first kind of cancer Des had had either. Brandt didn't know about the testicular cancer, because Des had been ashamed and embarrassed.

"As if he'd brought it on himself," Andy muttered. "Stop thinking about the past." There was no use in it, unless he was going to learn from it, which he had. Settling down was a dream he wanted very much to attain. He didn't have a sick brother to watch over and care for. Ty was already being kept from him because of God knew what—Brandt's jealousy, his hatred and possibly even his homophobia.

Though Andy knew Brandt had gay friends, ones who even had children, and he never said a bad word about them, at least not around Andy. He sure hadn't hesitated to point out that Andy was a slut, though.

Andy went to his duffle bag and took out a pair of shorts. He put them on then set about ordering their dinner. If he had his way, he and Salt wouldn't be leaving the hotel room until they both had to head to work Monday morning. Andy intended to indulge every one of their fantasies, and maybe find a few neither of them had known they had.

The beer was nice and cold in the cooler. Andy had stocked it up with ice before going to pick up Salt. He listened to the sounds Salt made as he showered and thought he could get used to hearing them every day, used to showering with the man, too.

Losing Destry and Ty had shown him how valuable love was. Granted, he wasn't there yet with Salt, but he wanted to be, eventually. Andy wanted the stability and the comfort of knowing someone would be there just for him, and he missed being the support for someone else.

Andy found the number to a pizza place that would deliver. He ordered two pizzas then settled onto the bed as the shower was shut off. Andy listened to the sounds of Salt finishing up in the bathroom, and in short order, Salt was standing in the doorway with a towel slung around his narrow hips.

"Forgot to grab clothes."

Andy arched an eyebrow at him. "I remember mentioning that I intended to keep you nekkid."

Salt looked delighted at the reminder. "You did say something about that. Just thought you wouldn't want the pizza delivery person to get an eyeful." Salt whipped the towel off and tossed it behind him.

"Jesus," Andy rasped, his gaze going to the long, fat erection Salt was sporting. "You are unbelievably perfect."

"Far from it," Salt muttered. "I don't have a perfect spot on my body."

"Perfect for me," Andy clarified. "Everything about you flips all my switches. I wish I could do that now."

Salt held up one finger. "Hey, I meant to ask. You were talking about organic stuff and all. I'm surprised you eat pizza now that I think about it."

Andy propped himself up a bit more comfortably. "As much as I can, I eat organic, but I don't think splurging hurts anything. Moderation is the key, except when it comes to me getting my hands on you."

"You can get your hands on me now," Salt offered, glancing down at his cock.

"As much as I'd love to, the pizza will be here shortly." Andy patted the bed. "Why don't you grab a couple of beers and come sit beside me. I'll let you pick out what we watch."

Salt's crooked smile sent all kinds of arousal zinging through Andy. It didn't matter to him why this one particular man was so appealing to him, he was just glad it was so.

Once Salt settled on the bed beside him, Andy had trouble even looking at the TV. There was all that naked, gorgeous man stretched out just begging for him to touch. Granted, Salt didn't actually beg out loud, but the erection he sported made his desire obvious.

When Andy was just about ready to throw in the towel and reach for Salt, there was a knock on the door. "Saved by the pizza delivery," he murmured to a smug-looking Salt. "You know you were driving me crazy."

Salt bobbed his head. "Was trying to. I want you to fuck me, and I don't want to wait."

Andy was rethinking his plan to wait, too. Why should he make them both suffer, when they wanted each other so much?

"Throw the blanket over your bits," he advised as he approached the door. He didn't intend to let the delivery person know Salt was there, but better safe than sorry. Andy grabbed his wallet and took out some cash. He opened the door and immediately stepped in the doorway hoping to keep his business private.

The delivery person was a young lady who was snapping her gum as she took the pizzas from the warmers. "That'll be twenty-six forty-two," she told him.

Andy thrust the money at her as he took the pizzas in his other hand. "Keep the change. Thanks."

"Yeah, thanks!" She bounded off like a happy puppy, her brown ponytail swinging back and forth. Andy stepped back and shut the door. He turned to set the pizzas on the table. Salt stood, his cock swaying from the movement.

"I want you," Salt said in a gruff tone. "Now, please."

Andy left the pizzas behind as he took a step towards Salt. He stopped long enough to remove his shorts, then he closed the distance between them.

"Just so you know, I'm probably going to screw up along the way, be a jerk at times, but I won't fuck around. I won't put you in jeopardy, or our relationship." He didn't know where the words came from as he wrapped his arms around Salt. His heart, was his best guess. "Be patient with me?"

Salt laughed softly and cupped his jaw. "I imagine we'll both fuck up plenty, seeing as we haven't done anything like this before. I won't screw around, either. I'll be patient, and I hope you will too."

It wasn't a declaration of undying love, but it was intense, true, something Andy would never forget or take for granted. He canted his head and pressed his lips to Salt's.

Salt opened for him like a flower greeting the sunlight. Sweet, minty, his tongue slicked alongside of Andy's, flicking, teasing.

Andy growled and jerked Salt closer, so close they could hardly draw breaths. He fisted his hand in the back of Salt's hair, holding him still and taking command of the kiss.

Lips, teeth, tongue—Andy used them all to bring Salt to a quaking state of need. Salt's dick leaked precum against Andy's lower belly. Andy got a handful of Salt's ass and squeezed, needing to mark this man as he had no other. When Salt moaned and turned his head aside, gasping, his chest heaving, Andy went after that sweet skin beneath his right ear.

"Fuck," Salt dragged out brokenly. "Andy, Jesus." He held onto Andy's biceps, arching his neck more for him.

Andy sucked up a dark mark that probably wouldn't be hidden by Salt's hair. He licked down farther, to the base of his neck, and left a matching hickey there.

Then he bent and took one turgid nipple between his lips and bit.

Salt bellowed, but he pressed Andy's head against his chest, so Andy knew it wasn't pain that drove that sound. He found Salt's other nipple with one hand and twirled the tip between his thumb and forefinger while nibbling on the other tit.

Salt rutted against him, grunting, loosing unintelligible words. Andy increased the pressure on Salt's nipples as much as he dared. Salt arched his back as if to pull away, but he kept a grip on Andy's nape, bringing him along for the ride.

Andy grinned and sucked up a pretty mark on each of Salt's pecs.

And before Salt could get another grunt out, he stood up fully and spun Salt around. "Hands on the table," he snarled.

Salt's skin pebbled with goose bumps as the man did as he'd been told. "It's fucking hot when you do that," Salt admitted.

"Glad you like it." Andy patted Salt's hip. "Spread and let me at that ass."

Salt moaned and dropped his head down as he spread his legs open. He bent over the table and lowered his chest down, so that his buttocks were higher than his shoulders.

Andy liked the view, very much. He traced the length of Salt's spine, first with his fingers, then his tongue. Salt shivered and made more of those deliciously needy sounds.

As Andy began layering kisses across Salt's cheeks, he reached between Salt's legs and hefted his heavy sack in his hand.

Salt whimpered and spread his legs farther. Andy licked the top of his crack, then left a purple mark there, too.

"Please, Andy," Salt rasped. "You're killing me."

"Loving on you," he corrected, then panicked when he feared Salt might take that to mean more than it did.

But Salt was right on track. "Torturing me, you mean. I need you!"

Andy gave Salt's nuts a little tug then left them alone so he could spread Salt's cheeks apart. He licked down the slightly fuzzy trail to the tightly furled hole nestled between them.

Andy moaned as he began rimming Salt. There was the taste of soap, for the most part, but he thought he could detect the faintest trace of his man's musky flavour, too.

Salt leant forward, settling more of his torso on the table. Andy moved forward, too, not letting that little pucker get out of reach. He buried his face in Salt's crease and let go of his cheeks in order to reach around and fist his dick.

"Yes," Salt hissed, then he keened as Andy gently scraped his teeth over Salt's hole. "Do that again."

Andy licked the wrinkled folds then used his teeth before nudging the tiny opening with his tongue. The moan Salt made sounded like it came up from his core, deep and soul-felt.

The way that pucker clenched around his tongue had Andy's cock aching to be inside Salt's griping channel. Andy pushed his tongue in as deep as he could get it, then curled it to tease the inner rim.

Salt began to curse a blue streak, unusual as far as Andy knew. He liked it, though, liked knowing he was driving Salt past all restraint.

Andy lightly stroked Salt's cock while tonguing his hole repeatedly. When he pushed a finger in alongside it, Salt's entire lower body quivered. Andy leant back, wanting to watch as he fingered Salt's ass. The way Salt's ring clenched around his knuckle was amazing, the grip so tight.

Salt's opening was wet and slick, so Andy worked a second finger in, then a third. Inner walls rippled and flexed, massaging his digits and Andy could hardly wait to feel them around his cock. Despite having come earlier, he wouldn't last long, not with the milking his shaft would get.

He curled his fingers and found Salt's gland. At the same time, he thumbed over the wet tip of Salt's dick.

"Fuck!" Salt shouted loudly enough that everyone in the motel likely heard it. Andy grinned and rubbed that spot again and again, until his own need grew too great for any more teasing.

"I'm gonna make love to you," Andy gritted out as he pulled his fingers from that hot sheath. His cheeks burned as embarrassment washed over him at having said those words, but he meant them. He meant the next ones, too. "Then I'm gonna fuck you and fuck you…"

"Please, do it." Salt moved restlessly. Andy gripped his shoulders.

"Come on. I told you, I want to see you when I take you." He helped Salt stand up and move over to lie on the bed. "I want to kiss you, watch you." The words came of their own accord as they'd been doing around Salt. Andy didn't want to keep them back, much. He wanted to be able to share how he felt with Salt, it was just difficult not to blush like a virgin seeing his first dick.

Salt bent his legs, getting his heels almost against his ass. He opened his arms up. "Come here. I could do with a kiss now."

"Gotta get this first, then I'll kiss you as much as you want me to." Andy's hands shook as he plucked the lube out of his bag.

"That might be a long, long time, sugar."

Andy snapped his gaze to Salt's upon hearing the endearment. "Sugar?" The way Salt had said it, so softly, yet full of affection… "I like that."

Salt beamed at him. "Good, thought you were going to object there for a second."

"Never." Andy tossed the lube onto the bed then bent to kiss Salt. At the same time, he got up onto the bed as well, manoeuvring himself over Salt.

The kiss was gentle, telling, laying both of them bare. They were in it together, the relationship, and the promises spoken and implied therein.

Salt cradled his nape, and Andy touched Salt's cheek, his neck, his shoulders. He wanted to feel every bit of his lover's body, learn every tiny spot that elicited pleasure.

Salt wiggled beneath him. Andy lowered his hips, wedging his cock against Salt's balls and ass. He rocked there, his tip nudging Salt's hole as they kissed. Salt wrapped his legs around Andy's hips. He pulled up into each gentle thrust, and before long, the need between them brought the kiss to an end as they each gasped and moaned.

Andy just had to rock into that warm embrace a few more times, then he felt around for the lube. He locked gazes with Salt. "I want you, so bad."

"You got me." Salt let his legs drop open again before he caught each one behind the knee and pulled them to his shoulders. "Come on. Show me what making love is."

Twin dots of deep red appeared on Salt's cheeks. Andy wasn't the only one shy about expressing his thoughts and needs. It was nice that they would learn to do so together.

Andy pushed up to his knees and opened the lube. He darted glances between his fingers and Salt's intense stare as he began stretching Salt's pucker with two fingers.

"More," Salt demanded after a few thrusts. "Give me more, sugar."

"I'll give you anything you want when you use that voice to ask," Andy informed Salt. There was never a sexier sound than that lust-thickened tone.

Salt moaned and his eyelids slid shut as Andy inserted a third finger into that tight opening. He had to bite back a whimper as he imagined his dick pushing in there. He caressed Salt's gland, delighted when it caused a bead of pre-cum to drip from his slit.

"Don't tease," Salt grumped. "Just get me ready and put your cock where we both want it."

"Patience," Andy murmured.

Salt opened one eye. "Patience ain't happening. I'm gonna come like a geyser here shortly, and I'd rather do that with your dick in me than with your fingers."

"Well, as that's what I want, too..." Andy pulled his fingers free and slicked up his shaft. Salt pulled his legs up a little more, offering his stretched hole. "Beautiful."

Salt snorted. "I don't know about that — oh." He broke off on a long moan as Andy nudged his cock head against the slicked skin. "More of that, please."

Andy made sure he had his dick lined up right, then he dropped down onto his elbows over Salt as he began pushing into the tightest, hottest grip he'd ever experienced. Andy was aware part of the difference was emotional. Probably a huge part.

Salt released his legs as Andy sank his cock in deeper. Salt's blissful expression would forever be etched in Andy's mind. Parted lips, slack mouth, eyes all but closed and soft, wanton sounds — Salt was the image of ecstasy.

Andy lowered himself more and kissed those parted lips, slipping his tongue right on in and laying claim to Salt's mouth. Salt clutched at his arms, sucking on his tongue a moment later when Andy thrust in the last few inches.

Salt rolled his head aside and a low, guttural sound spilled from his lips. Andy held still until Salt turned his head again and peered up at him. There were no words to be said, none Andy could think of as he began a slow, grinding movement of his hips.

The gripping heat around his cock was exquisite. Those inner walls rippled and worked his length with each drive in. They tried to hold his shaft in place as he withdrew, and— *Oh God, it's so fucking perfect. He's perfect, for me.*

Andy struggled to keep his eyes open as he filled Salt again and again. Salt watched him through narrowly slitted lids, the gleam of his dark eyes barely discernible. Andy took kisses when he could, losing himself in the feel and taste of his lover.

The rhythmic spasming of Salt's inner walls increased in speed and intensity. Andy shuddered as he began to drive in faster, harder. He nipped at Salt's lips, then his jaw. Salt moved like a dancer beneath him, an erotic fantasy come to life.

Andy had to have more, had to have everything Salt would give him. Shouting, he slammed into Salt, driving him across the mattress with each jarring thrust. Salt matched him in fierceness, bellowing and curling his fingers against Andy's skin, scoring him with blunt fingernails.

It drove Andy to reach for more. He crushed his mouth to Salt's and lost some of his rhythm for a moment. Salt keened and Andy leaned up, working harder, wanting in so deep that Salt could never be free of him.

Salt shoved a hand between them, his knuckles rubbing Andy's belly. Friction there told him exactly what Salt was doing, and Andy wished he could see everything, every part of Salt.

But his vision hazed as his balls drew tight. "Salt," he got out.

"Yeah." Salt arched his neck, his entire body going tight but no part as tight as the heat gripping Andy's dick. Salt bucked as cum shot from his cock. Andy could smell it, that musky scent of spunk, and combined with the feel of those inner walls around his shaft, it pulled his climax right out of him.

He shoved in once, twice, then hammered his hips against Salt's ass in short thrusts as he pumped his release into Salt. Every jet of seed felt like it burst forth from the deepest part of him, turning him inside out with a rapturous feeling.

When he finally finished coming, Andy could hardly hold himself up. Then he didn't have to, because Salt was pulling him down.

"Come here," Salt grumbled. "Rest. Stay in there."

Andy almost laughed at that, but he knew what Salt meant. He didn't want their connection to end either. So he gingerly lowered himself on top of Salt, and revelled in being held by his lover.

Chapter Thirteen

That tickles. Salt cracked open one eye and his sleep-befuddled brain wondered what in the hell was making his ass itch. After a few seconds, some things became very clear. Namely, that Andy was asleep and lying halfway on him, and that was Andy's cum trickling out his hole making Salt want to squirm and scratch.

"Be still, pillow," Andy groused when Salt tried to get a hand to his backside. He kind of wanted to just feel that for himself...with something other than his twitchy hole.

"Your spunk's leaking out and making me wiggle," he told Andy.

Andy raised his head and blinked slowly. "Huh?"

Oh, hell, the man was adorable with his hair sticking up every which way and that totally confused expression on.

"You came in my ass, and it's coming back out now," Salt explained slowly. "Do you have any idea how that feels? Like spiders—"

Andy shoved himself up to an uncomfortable-looking sitting position as he waved his hands in front of Salt. "No, stop! Comparing my cum to spiders is wrong on more levels than I can even comprehend!"

Salt snickered. He guessed that was kind of...wrong. "Well, it tickles and I was trying to take care of that."

Andy arched an eyebrow. "I could take care of that?"

Salt tried to figure out what the catch was, because there was something sneaky in Andy's expression. "You're going to get me a wash cloth?"

Andy shook his head. "Oh no, baby. You just roll over and leave it all to me."

Salt froze for a second, catching on finally. Then he rolled over so fast and put his ass up in the air that he couldn't have been more than a blur.

Andy's laughter came right before Andy's hands spreading his cheeks. "Looks amazing, Salt. Like me and you." Then Andy licked and Salt's brain plumb shorted out. "Mm, got to do this every chance I get."

Salt couldn't articulate how much he agreed with that idea. Not when Andy was rimming him and cleaning his own cum off and out of Salt.

By the time Andy was done, Salt's cock was hard and he was close enough that when Andy flipped him over and immediately sucked Salt's glans into his mouth, Salt didn't even last beyond the first flick of tongue. His balls ached with the force of his release. It'd been years since Salt had come so many times in one day.

"Now I have us both in me," Andy said when he sat up. His cock was erect, and Salt was trying to find the energy to reach for it when Andy's phone blared an obnoxious tune. "Fuck you, Brandt."

"That's your brother?" Salt asked, waking up a bit more and debating whether or not to dive for the phone.

"It is, and I already turned everything in I need to. He knows I'm taking the weekend off, so he can just find someone else to bitch at." Andy licked his lips. "I have plans for you, man."

Salt propped himself up on his elbows. He hated to bring it up, but... "What if he's calling for something important? Maybe something to do with Ty?"

Andy shook his head, sadness flitting across his features. "No. He wouldn't tell me, because that would imply he thought I had a right to know. I only found out about Ty breaking his arm last year because one of Brandt and Mary's kids told me."

"Your nieces or nephews?" Salt prodded.

Andy huffed and glared at the phone. "No. I mean, I would love for them to be, but Brandt and Mary have told them we aren't related. They'll figure it out someday, maybe."

"That's really fucked up, Andy. How'd that work when Brandt was playing nice?"

"His kids were always doing something," Andy explained. "Sports, music lessons, avoidance training..."

Salt snorted. "Yeah I think maybe it might be best if I never met—" Andy's phone started up again. "Brandt."

"Wish I hadn't ever met him." Andy grabbed his phone and silenced it somehow, Salt couldn't tell what he'd done. Andy set the phone back on the night stand. "There. Now he can just—"

Andy went still, eerily so as he stared at the phone. Salt bolted up and sat beside him. "What? What's wrong?"

"It's a trick." Andy picked the phone up again. "Brandt's fucking with me."

"Can I see?" Salt held out his hand.

Andy put his phone in it after tapping the screen and bringing up a text message. "He says Ty is missing. Why would he even tell me if that was true? He's fucking with me."

The phone began to ring, no tone to it, but the name and number coming up on the screen. "What if he's not?"

Andy took the phone. "I think he is but—" He answered the call. "Ty is not missing. You're just fucking with me because—" Andy shut his mouth and paled.

Salt couldn't hear what Brandt was saying, but Andy's lips thinned down to invisible and he began to shake.

"You're full of shit! I said he's not missing because you're lying to me, not because he's with me!" Andy snapped. "I'm in Montana with my boyfriend, and only my boyfriend. Ty isn't here and never has been." Andy took a deep breath and closed his eyes. "Now listen closely to me. This isn't funny. It's not a show of your power over me. It's sick, and I will have a lawyer so far up your ass tomorrow you can French-kiss him. I've had enough of this shit from you."

Andy looked shocked, and Salt could only guess it was at his own words since he was still blasting Brandt. From what Salt had gathered, and what Andy had said, he'd given up on ever having any place in Ty's life.

But it sure sounded like something had broken in Andy and let loose a lion. He roared more than once at his brother before telling him, "I'll be knocking at your door in a few hours. You'd better answer. And call the police." Andy listened then growled before uttering in a fierce tone, "I don't *care* how it makes you look to them or anyone else, and neither should you. Ty and Ty alone should be your only concern."

Whatever Brandt said to that infuriated Andy. Anger shuttered his features as he hung up the phone. His face was flushed and there was tic having a wild time beneath his jaw.

"I have to go. I'm sorry but—"

Salt cut Andy off with a grunt and a gesture. "Don't be sorry. Someone has to care about your nephew, and it doesn't sound like Brandt is gonna be that someone."

Andy ground his teeth, the sound of it making the fine hairs on Salt's nape quiver. "You know what he said before I hung up on him?"

Salt shook his head. "No."

"He said Ty was more trouble than he was worth, even with the stocks." Andy stood up, his hands fisted. "If anything happens to Ty, Brandt will try to claim his share of the company."

Standing, Salt asked a question he didn't want to even think possible. "Would he do something to get Ty out of the way?"

Andy jerked his head up, his complexion draining of almost all colour. "No," he whispered. "He wouldn't. I don't think he would. I don't know." Andy shook his head. "No, even Brandt isn't that big of a scumbag. More than likely, he and Ty argued about something. Ty's been through hell with his daddy dying and me disappearing out of his life, even though I wanted to see him. I was stupid for handing him over."

"Did you sign papers?" Salt prodded. "Or did Destry leave a will asking that you raise Ty?"

"He asked that Brandt and I do what was best for Ty, always," Andy said. "I think Brandt had been working him, too, and Destry wanted to believe Brandt had changed. Needed to believe it. There wasn't a specific appointment for guardianship. And yeah, I signed something, but Brandt never gave me a copy. Every time I ask him about it, he refuses to tell me. I should have gotten a lawyer, I know, but I'd hoped that Ty was happy with him."

There wasn't much to say to that. Salt knew Andy was kicking himself for being so gullible, and Salt couldn't tell him he hadn't been. He could point out that Brandt was a manipulative asshole, but Andy knew that too.

"You should get a lawyer, as soon as possible," he suggested after a moment. "See what your rights are, and if Brandt can keep you from Ty like he's been doing. Maybe even get some kind of in-home study done to see if Ty's being treated right and if he's happy."

Andy canted his head, hope lighting his eyes. "You think that can be done?"

Salt nodded. "I don't see why not. Ty's safety and happiness should be the priorities, and I'd think having that checked into, especially in light of him running away — if that's what he's done — would be necessary. Cops might even turn the information over to whatever child welfare agency there is."

Andy scrubbed his hands over his face. "Okay. Okay, yeah." He reached for Salt. "Man, I don't want to leave you but—"

"Go on, take care of your business and your family. I'll still be here when you come back." Salt ached for Andy already, but the man had to get this whole situation with Ty and Brandt under control. Salt held

Andy's chin so he could take a gentle kiss, then he stepped back. "I'll help you get your stuff ready."

"Stay here if you want. I paid for the weekend."

Salt waved off the offer. "Maybe they'll give you a refund if you tell them it's a family emergency, explain about Ty. I don't want to stay here without you."

"Not even until morning, so you can sleep a while?" Andy asked as he began getting dressed.

"Nah," Salt murmured, watching the way all those sexy muscles moved. "Sleep better in my own bed if I'm not gonna be sleeping with you."

"Be careful driving home." Andy buttoned and zipped his jeans. He looked at Salt. "I don't want a deer trying to wreck your truck."

Salt had to laugh at that. "Yeah, me neither. Last time that happened the airbag went off and knocked the bejeezus out of me. It sucked."

"Tends to be worse than the wreck sometimes." Andy stopped in the middle of buttoning his shirt. "I don't know how long this will take me, Salt. If... I might have to... What if I have to stay away? Because you know how bigoted some people can be here, and if there's a court case—"

God, that broke Salt's heart, but he wouldn't ever make Andy choose between him and Ty. "You do what you have to do. I'll be here when you come back," he repeated. "Just have faith in that, in me."

Andy gave him a lopsided smile. "I will. It's just a lot to ask."

Salt canted his head as if considering it. "Nope," he declared. "That's having a relationship, I think. You do things for each other, and trust each other."

"And love each other," Andy said quietly.

Salt's heart must have stopped because he went numb from head to toe.

Andy turned the full force of his gaze on him. "I don't know for sure what our kind of love feels like. I know how to love family, and things, but I've never had the kinds of feelings I have for you before. This is… It's bigger than any words I can find. Right here." Andy put his hand over his heart. "I feel you here, and leaving makes this spot ache. I don't want to go, but I have to."

Salt swallowed, did it again before he could speak. "I understand. We'll get to where we're meant to be, as long as we hang on to each other. Even if that means only by phone until this is all straightened out." He moved closer and put his hand over Andy's. "Mine's right here with yours. That's why it feels like your heart's too big for your chest. You have mine, too."

It was sappy, and maybe downright silly, but it was the truth. Andy had his heart.

Andy kissed him again, deep, devouring, tinged with lingering sadness. Then he finished dressing and packed up the few things he'd got out. Salt got his gear together as well, and he grabbed the pizzas they hadn't even eaten. "Take one, eat it on the road if you get hungry."

"Be safe, Salt." Andy's eyes looked to be watering.

Salt's sure as hell burned too. "You too, sugar. I'm here when you need me, anytime."

Watching Andy drive away hurt like having a tooth pulled, but Salt knew it had to be done. He wanted Andy happy, and that wasn't going to happen with the way things were currently going with Andy's family.

Salt racked his brain, trying to think of something to do to help Andy. It wasn't until he was almost home that he remembered his bosses had friends in high places—namely an ex-FBI agent and some police officers. Granted, they were all in Texas, but maybe they could at least give Andy some advice.

Everyone was asleep when he quietly entered the bunkhouse. Salt was restless, wanting to get on with grovelling for help if that was what it took. But there was nothing he could do until everyone else was up and alert.

He sent Andy a short text, because he couldn't just go to sleep without doing that first.

Be safe, and remember, I'm here for you.

Salt went to sleep with gritty eyes and an ache in his heart.

Chapter Fourteen

Andy pounded on Brandt's door. Brandt opened it immediately, which Andy took to mean he'd been waiting right inside, had probably even heard Andy pull up.

"What have you found out?" Andy snapped as Brandt averted his eyes. "Did you call the cops?"

Brandt nodded. "Yeah, they've been here and gone. Said Ty's one of dozens of runaways they'll keep an eye out for."

Andy wasn't sure he trusted Brandt, which was a horrible way to feel about his own sibling, but there it was. He'd tried to get along with Brandt, but nothing he'd done made the man like him. There'd be no more playing Brandt's game for Andy.

"Did they leave a card to call them at, whoever's in charge of the case?" he asked.

Brandt's features got that pinched look to them like they did when he was on the verge of losing his temper. "You think I'm lying?"

Andy shrugged. "I think you've been lying about a lot of things, and it's fixing to stop."

"Fuck you," Brandt snarled. "All I wanted was to keep Ty from being like you and Destry!"

Andy reeled back a half step in the face of Brandt's shouting. "Like us how? Brothers who took care of one another?"

"Took care of one another, right." Brandt sneered. "You and Destry were always too close, but no one else seemed to notice it."

Andy's stomach heaved and he prayed he'd got the wrong impression of Brandt's words, that he was just jealous of Andy and Destry's brotherly relationship.

"Don't even deny it," Brandt continued, his voice dripping with disgust. "I know he was bi, and once you moved in with him and Ty, Destry never dated anyone again. Neither did you, so—"

"You're the sick one in this family," Andy said, wondering how Brandt had got so twisted. "How you can conclude that something…something like that was going on is beyond me. Destry didn't date because he was embarrassed about losing a testicle to cancer! The idea of a fake one, a prosthetic one, scared him. Why? I don't know. He didn't know, but he told me he'd lost all sexual desire anyway. And he was always sick, almost always. He had Ty, he was happy, you asshole. Ty was happy, too. But your filthy mind can't comprehend a loving, familial relationship, could it? No," he ground out. "No, don't open your god damned mouth because if you say one more perverted thing, I'll be introducing your teeth to my fist. You just shut up and expect me to kick back from now on."

Andy had to struggle not to punch Brandt, and it looked like Brandt was trying to restrain himself as well. Andy didn't expect the punch that Brandt threw and barely managed to dodge it.

"It was always you and him," Brandt muttered as Andy tried to block the second punch. "Always you two. I was never good enough, or fun enough, or bad enough, whatever."

Andy got his arms around Brandt, locking Brandt's down at his sides. "Bullshit. We tried to include you, but you never wanted anything to do with us until Destry was dying. You hated us from the get-go."

"Whatever." Brandt bucked and stomped on Andy's right foot. "I hate you!"

"I know." Andy's anger died away in an instant and he let Brandt go, shoving him back to prevent himself from getting hit. "I know you do, and I'm sorry. I'd have loved to have two brothers."

Brandt muttered something Andy decided to pretend he didn't hear. Andy turned and walked out of his brother's house, possibly for the last time.

With all the hatred Brandt had spewed, Andy wondered what he'd told Ty. Nothing as filthy as what he'd accused Andy of. Ty would know it wasn't true, anyway. Ty had lived with Des and Andy for the first thirteen years of his life. He'd been old enough to spot anything unnatural like that.

But Brandt undoubtedly had used other lies, and Andy had been complacent about it all. It'd been easier not to fight, easier to believe Ty would be happy with Brandt.

Because thinking he wasn't meant Andy would have to face the fact that he'd been a total fool. Andy was facing that fact now. He'd let Brandt manipulate him for far too long. Destry had wanted them to do what was best for Ty, and Andy was damn well going to do that.

Hopefully he wasn't too late.

* * * *

"She's so beautiful." Rocky sighed and Salt tried really hard not to roll his eyes.

"She's straight," he said for what might have been the hundredth time. "Jen's not into chicks."

Rocky grimaced then took a sip of her coffee. She set the cup back down. "You don't have to be a Sour Saltie just because your guy's tangled up with family shit. I know you miss him, but don't be a dick to me."

"Oh, my God," Salt muttered as he tried not to pull his hair out. "Rocky, I'm not being a dick. I'm trying to get you to see what's right in front of your face. Jen's a nice lady and all, but she doesn't flirt back with you or anything. I just want you to be happy with someone who loves and appreciates the person that you are."

Rocky glowered at him for a moment then went back to sipping her coffee. Salt figured she'd at least listened to him, and wasn't calling him a dick again.

"Have you heard any news from Andy?" she asked him a few minutes later, a sign that she was over the squabble and ready to make peace. "They still haven't found his nephew?"

Salt bit his lip to combat the pain that came when he thought of Andy, alone and trying to deal with the disaster happening in his life. "Nope. It's been a week, and everyone's getting more and more worried. Well, Brandt might not be. Andy don't know since his lawyer has advised him to cut off contact with his twisted sib."

"He is pretty damned twisted," Rocky agreed. "Couldn't believe that shit when you told me at first. Then I thought about some of the ignorant people I've met, ones who think anyone in the rainbow will fuck anyone else in it, regardless of everything. There's some sick bastards in this world, for sure. Seems to me the homophobes have the dirtiest minds ever created."

"Maybe. There's plenty who bitch that bisexual people just want more opportunities to get laid, so they take whatever gender they can get." He shook his head. "Man, I never understood that kind of thinking. Always figured being bi was a lucky thing to be. Meant you could love someone because of who they were, not what parts they had. I'm hardwired to like dick and only that."

"Same for me and pussy," Rocky said. "Don't cringe when I say that word."

"Sorry. My mama would have tanned my hide for using it, though, whereas she didn't care so much about the names for guy parts. She said women deserved more respect after all the crap they put up with." He smiled at the memory.

Rocky widened her eyes at him. "Oh my hell, your mama sounds like my dream woman! Smart, tough, demanding — yeah, I'd love her like crazy."

"Love who like crazy?" Jen said, stopping beside their table.

Salt frowned at the brittle voice she used. Normally she didn't seem to be so on edge. Jen kept her eyes on her order pad.

"Huh?" Rocky wiped her mouth. "Oh. Er, I was just..." She stopped talking and her sneaky look slipped into place. Jen might not have recognised it, but Rocky had been his friend long enough that he knew her moods. "Just talking about a woman, you wouldn't know her."

"I might." Jen tapped the pen to the pad.

"I doubt it. She's not from around here."

It was on the verge of Salt's tongue to inform Jen that the 'she' in question was no longer of this Earth, either. His mama had passed away a long time ago. Rocky kicked him under the table. Salt got the hint to keep his mouth shut.

"I've been other places," Jen pressed, finally looking at Rocky.

Rocky hitched up one shoulder. "I think I'll have a slice of whatever pie you're serving today."

Jen looked fit to break the nearest object for a split second, then her fake smile slid into place. "Okay. What would you like, Salt?"

"Burger and fries, the usual," he told her. "And a glass of tea."

"I'll be right back with your orders." Jen turned and it sure looked like there was a little bit of extra swing to her hips.

"Is she doing that on purpose?" Salt had to ask.

Rocky broke out in a huge grin. "Hell yeah. Told you she isn't uninterested in me. She's jealous."

"Of a dead woman?" he had to ask.

Rocky crossed her eyes at him. "She doesn't know the lady in question is dead—and by the way, I totally mean that about your mom. I'd be chasing her like a hungry dog chasing a rabbit."

Salt instantly reverted to age eight. "Gross."

Rocky laughed at him and he flipped her off. That just made her even happier, and he leant back in the booth to glare at her.

"Here's your orders," Jen said. "Manny knows you well, Salt. He had your burger going as soon as you walked in." She set the meal in front of him, along with his glass of tea. Then she turned to Rocky. "Here's today's pie—sweet potato. It's delicious."

Salt just about fell out of his seat at the way Jen purred those last two words. Had he been wrong about Jen? It sure seemed that way.

Jen left them alone and Salt bowed his head. "Go ahead and say it."

"You were wrong," Rocky sang with entirely too much glee. "Wrong, wrong, wrong. You should know men are always wrong when they argue with a woman. It's like a universal truth."

"Should have remembered that one. Mama told me it, too." Salt took a huge bite of his burger and moaned. There just was nothing else like a real homemade burger done right. The diner didn't use pre-shaped patties, not with all the ranchers coming in to eat. They'd have been run out of town if they'd tried it.

"This pie is fucking awesome." Rocky did her own version of the food-bliss moan.

They ate quickly and just as they stood to leave, Salt's phone went off with the chime for Andy's ringtone.

Rocky made shooing gestures with her hands. "I've got the bill this time. It'll give me a chance to talk to Jen, hopefully. You buy the next one."

Salt answered the phone as he made his way out of the diner. "Hey, what's up? Anything new?" He'd promised to wait, and he would, but that didn't mean he didn't wish for Andy to get Ty and come back to him. That wasn't even possible, considering Andy's job, but they'd figure something out.

"Not much. I hired a private detective recommended to me by your boss, Will. Thanks for that."

"You're welcome. I'm just glad he could help, or knew someone else who could help." Salt had the best bosses. "And the lawyer?"

"I told you I met your bosses' employers when I was in Texas?" Andy asked.

Salt thought back. "No, I don't think you did. Probably you were going to share that on our weekend."

"I think so. They're good people, too. Anyway, one of them contacted a guy they know who used to be a lawyer here in Montana. A James Stratton. Him and his husband actually flew out here to meet with me. Stratton seems kind of skittish, but he's smart, and he's angry on mine and Ty's behalf. I think he can do anything he tells me he can."

Salt stepped outside and into a shady spot against the front of the diner. "What's he told you he can do so far?"

"That Ty is old enough to choose where he wants to live, and that he's going to go after Brandt for psychological abuse and neglect at the very least, if Ty wants to live with me and Brandt fights us." Andy sighed. "I hope it doesn't come to that, but Brandt is... He's a fucking mess. I don't think even dropping him on his head as a baby could have made him like this."

"Was he really dropped?"

Andy chuckled. "No, but maybe if he had been, he'd be nicer."

"Maybe," Salt agreed. "No news on Ty?"

"The PI is talking to his friends, but it's hard since Ty didn't have a cell phone or access to the Internet at home. Welsh, that's the PI, she seems to think that Ty would be easily traced if he'd had either of those things. Last I heard, she's trying to get into the Internet files of the one place he did have access."

Salt felt his eyebrows arch up almost to his hairline. "You mean—" He bit off the rest of that. If the PI was breaking into the school's records—the only place Salt could think of where Ty would have had access, except maybe at friends' houses—then he didn't want to know.

"Yeah, I didn't ask, either. I have to believe he's okay, Salt. I have to."

"He is." Salt believed that. He thought Ty was hurting from his daddy's death and, though he wouldn't say so to Andy, from Andy's handing him over so easily, not to mention Brandt's nasty everything. "He's gonna be fine."

Rocky came out the door, smiling fit to be tied. She waved at him then pointed to the feed store.

"Go on," he told her. "I'll walk down there."

"You and Rocky in town?" Andy asked him.

"Yeah, feed run. Seems our organic food for the horses has arrived."

"Good. Hey, someone's at the door. I better go."

Salt could hear the knocking. "Yeah, you do what you gotta do. I'll talk to you tonight." Maybe some phone sex would make them both feel a little better. If Salt could keep from laughing his ass off when he tried to talk dirty.

Salt sauntered down the sidewalk, thinking about everything—him, Andy, Ty, Salt's job—when his phone rang again. He answered it immediately. "Andy, everything okay?"

"No. Yes." Andy sobbed and Salt feared the worst, until he remembered the Yes part of that answer.

And the faint, crackly voice of a teenage boy came over the line. "Ty?"

"He's here, Salt. He's here. I just... He's talking to his friend, who brought him over. He's fine. I need to call my lawyer. See who he wants me to call after that."

"If there's anything I can do, sugar, you let me know. I can be on your doorstep in three hours." Salt would do it, too. He'd only got one day of the previous weekend off. His bosses would shove him down the road if they knew he wanted to go to Andy.

"I might take you up on that. God, it'd be so good to hold you. Oh! I have to go." Andy sounded happy and scared, and it killed Salt that he couldn't be there with him.

"I love you," he said, the words flowing smooth and sweet, like honey off his tongue.

"Damn it, cowboy, you know I love you too." Andy sniffled and Salt had to rub at his chest. "I'll call you later."

"When you can." Salt disconnected the call. He figured Andy might be busier than he expected to be later.

* * * *

Andy couldn't stop staring at Ty. He'd grown a lot since Andy had last seen him. Ty had to be almost six feet tall now, and he was thin in that gangly teenage boy way. At least, Ty hoped that was all it was.

"I'd like to talk to you," Ty said, turning from his friend, a boy who didn't look to be much older than him. Ty seemed determined and not like the happy, carefree child he'd been.

No surprise there. I practically handed him to the devil. "Okay. I need to call my lawyer—"

"No," Ty barked out. "No. I'll leave if you call anyone!"

Andy held up his hands in supplication. "All right. I won't—yet, but I'm not going to let you bully me any more than I'll let anyone else do so." He'd barely stopped himself from naming Brandt, but Stratton had told him bad-mouthing anyone around Ty could be cause for whoever was doing it to lose visitation or custody rights.

Andy hadn't been certain he'd get to see Ty again. He wasn't going to blow it now. "Can I... Can I hug you? Please? I've been so worried."

Ty tipped his chin up. "Why? You didn't seem to care about me once Dad died."

"That's not true," Andy said, aching to hold his nephew. "I never stopped loving you. You are like a son to me. I helped raise you—"

Ty sneered, looking so much like Brandt that Andy was shocked, but Brandt and Des had shared more than a passing resemblance. "And sent me to live with Brandt. You didn't want to keep me."

"I did too," Andy argued. He couldn't keep the tears from coming. "I did, but it was pointed out to me that I couldn't offer you a family—"

"You *were* my family!" Ty yelled, stomping one foot. "You were, and you left me!"

Andy had no comeback for that. It was the truth. He sank down onto the couch. "I did. I did because I thought it was best for you. I'm just a guy who never could settle down with a boyfriend. I never even had a boyfriend except for a few weeks in college. And now."

"So it was just me you didn't want. Was I gonna be in the way of all your screwing around?" The bitterness in Ty's voice was too much.

Andy swiped at the tears streaming down his cheeks. "Stop it. You aren't listening to me, and I need you to."

"Why should I?" Ty said with all the petulance of a fourteen-year-old.

"You're here, aren't you?" Andy gestured to the room. "Don't you want to talk about why that is?"

Ty bit his lip and glanced at his friend, who shrugged. Then he faced Andy again. "I can't believe you sent me to live with Brandt and Mary."

Andy didn't see a way around the whole truth, but he would try not to bash his brother and sister-in-law. "You remember how Mary took you into the other room after your dad passed away?"

Ty nodded, his eyes glistening.

"Brandt started telling me how you'd be better off with them. They had a house, with a yard, pets, kids, and I had nothing. Just me, and this place." Andy held up a hand when Ty looked like he was about to speak. "Please. Let me finish. Mary came back in the room without you. She told me you wanted to go home with them. The way she said it, I took it to mean to stay. I thought maybe you were mad at me because your dad died and I didn't."

"That's just stupid," Ty muttered.

Andy wasn't sure about that, but he let it go. "I didn't know."

Ty crossed his arms over his chest. He glared at Andy. "I didn't want to go with them at all. Mary told me you said I had to. Then after the funeral, they told me you wanted to be able to go out and do whatever, that you didn't want to raise a kid. I didn't understand why you hated me all of the sudden."

"I didn't," Andy assured him. "I told you, that day I waited for you outside your school."

"You did, but I'd had months of Brandt and Mary telling me how you were going out of town with one guy or another, and were too busy to talk to me on the phone or come by."

Andy's head almost exploded off his neck, just about popped right off. "That's all lies! I started making sales calls, and maybe sometimes when I was doing that, at night I might have, uh, went out to a club or two. That's not the same thing. I was *working*, trying to make this company something, for you."

Ty did cry then, quietly, as tears spilled onto his cheeks. "I'd rather have had you. I lost my home, my dad, my uncle — everything."

"I'm so sorry." Andy hadn't ever hurt so bad inside, not since losing Des. Maybe not even then. He'd had time to prepare for that. "I'm sorry. I was a fool. I was upset. I loved Des, you know that. I love you. Des dying, it ripped me up inside, and I agreed to things I should have thought of and talked to you about."

"They played you both," said Ty's friend. "Though you're the adult, dude. Not impressed with your brains."

"I'm not either," Andy told him. "Ty." He waited for Ty to look at him. "I need to know, did Brandt or Mary ever hurt you? Physically or emotionally?"

"Every time they told me you had forgotten about me," Ty said in a cracking voice. "Every time they told me you didn't want me. But not physically, no. They fed me, kept me clothed, all that, but there wasn't any hugging not long after I moved in there. No teasing, no laughing. I was there, like some prize they didn't want. Finally figured out they just wanted the shares to the company, the ones in my name. That's when I left."

"You heard them say that?" Andy enquired, sitting up a little straighter.

Ty bobbed his head as he twined his fingers together. "Yeah. They knew I could hear them, too, I think. I was in the kitchen and they were in the study across the hall. Doors were open. Maybe they thought I had my mp3 player going. Whatever, they just wanted me for those shares." Ty rubbed his eyes and sniffled. "And now I think maybe to hurt you."

"They hurt us both, but I never should have let it happen." Andy wanted to stand up, to reach for Ty and hold him. He wanted to make everything as right in Ty's world as he possibly could. "I should have been smarter, and fought for you. I should have seen past my grief and put you first. That I didn't, well, it sure makes it clear to me what kind of an asshole I was, but I'm not that guy anymore."

"You weren't ever an asshole," Ty told him. "You were maybe stupid for not seeing how much I needed you. Stupid for thinking I'd rather be with Brandt and Mary. Stupid for letting it go on so long—"

Andy refused to rise to the bait. Ty was right, anyway.

"But if you regret it, then fix it." Ty took a paper out of his shirt pocket. "Here's a number where you can reach me. It's a prepaid cell phone, and you're the only one who has the number." And with that, Ty turned and bounded for the door.

"Ty, wait!" Andy sprang up from the couch, but with the coffee table in the way, he couldn't catch Ty or his friend. Andy ran down the stairs after them, but the boys were gone by the time he hit the first floor. Panting, winded and miserable, he realised he still had the number in his hand.

Andy went to the elevators to get back to his place. The door was standing open, but he wasn't concerned that anyone would have intruded. He shut the door behind him but didn't lock it, just in case Ty wanted to come back.

"I should have given him Destry's keys." Andy popped himself on the forehead. "Damn it!"

He ran to the nearest window and pulled the blinds aside. Why hadn't he thought to see if the boys were in sight that way? They weren't, and he gave a disgruntled sigh as he let the blinds fall back in place.

Andy closed his eyes and pictured Ty. The boy had been hurting, so bad, and Andy needed to decide if he, as Ty's uncle, should even try to gain custody of Ty. After all, it was his fault Ty had ended up living with Brandt. If he'd just not had his head up his ass, if he'd seen through Brandt's manipulations— If he'd just talked to Ty in the first place.

He hadn't, he hadn't and all the self-castigation in the world wouldn't change that fact. Was he the right person to raise Ty? And what about Salt?

Andy sat back down on the couch and rested his head in his hands. There were so many decisions to make. Before he'd seen Ty today, he'd thought he was definitely the best person for Ty to live with, but knowing the pain he'd caused his nephew, Andy didn't see how Ty could ever forgive him.

Brandt wasn't an option, either.

Salt... Andy had to smile, thinking about the cowboy and Ty. He could just picture Salt teaching Ty the cowboy way. Something told Andy that Salt would make a great parent, or father figure. Ty would surely find peace of a sorts with someone like Salt guiding him.

Would Salt even want to raise a kid? Granted, Ty was fourteen, so legally there weren't many years' worth of raising left. Still, taking in a teenage boy, one who was no kin to him? Andy wondered what was wrong with him, thinking that way. He wasn't going to pawn Ty off on Salt!

Then the thought occurred to him. He didn't want Salt to raise Ty, he wanted Salt to help *him* bring Ty up to be the man he should be.

With a sudden clarity, he knew he wanted it all. The house, a dog or two, Ty and Salt. Maybe even a horse or three, depending on the size of their property.

Andy wanted that more than he wanted his company to succeed.

"It's not my company anymore," he reminded himself. He wouldn't be using Ty for his shares, either, which meant the majority of the company wasn't his. That was okay. Andy had always intended to sign his over to Ty once the boy was mature enough to handle the company.

Yet for all he knew, Ty might not want the company. Hadn't Ty just been yelling at him that he wanted his family? Or he had, back when Andy had acted like family.

Andy wanted to give Ty that family again. It wouldn't be the same, with Destry gone, but it'd be good. Really good, if Salt wanted them both. Taking Ty in would mean no more week-long sales trips. Andy could get down with that.

He thought about it for another half hour, waffling between calling the lawyer or Salt first. It shouldn't have been a difficult choice, but Andy couldn't seem to decide what he needed to do next. What he did know was that Salt made him a better man, not that Andy thought he'd ever been evil, exactly. Self-absorbed, certainly, but that had changed.

What he had to figure out, too, was if he could truly be the guardian Ty needed. There would be no more screwing up with his nephew, not on his part. And he needed to put Ty first. That meant deciding what was best for him. It certainly wasn't living with Brandt.

Andy loved his nephew, and would do anything for him. Giving him up had hurt, but he had only himself to blame for that. Now he needed to step up. As much as he loved Ty, Ty couldn't make all the decisions. Andy had to start, and hope that Ty would agree to live with him.

Which meant he was calling James Stratton first, because Andy wanted Ty. If Salt didn't want to help raise the boy, then as much as Andy would hate to, he'd have to break things off with Salt.

Chapter Fifteen

Salt wasn't a hundred per cent certain that showing up at Andy's apartment was the wisest thing to do, but there'd been so much worry in Andy's voice last night as they'd discussed Ty. He guessed Andy should be forgiven for not knowing how much Salt wanted to help him—be that with raising Ty, or not. Salt wanted Andy, and if Ty was included, then he was in.

Being a father had never really been something Salt had imagined for himself, and while he wouldn't be if Andy gained custody of Ty, he would be some sort of parental figure. Maybe. Salt wasn't sure.

There was no denying, not to himself, nor to Andy, that he was growing more and more excited about the opportunity. That was why Andy's fears that Salt wasn't on board with him had hurt so badly.

Andy was under a lot of stress, however, and he didn't need Salt's bitching about his feelings being stomped on and such. Salt was a big boy. He understood that Andy had to put Ty first. Every kid needed someone who was completely on their side.

So he told himself to put Ty first, too, and Andy. His own perceived snubbing was something he needed to get past. Andy had wronged Ty once, as much as Salt hated to admit it. There were reasons for it, sure, but the kid had been the one to suffer most.

There would be a lot for Andy to make up for, and Salt would be at his side, helping him. That Andy was terrified of not being stable enough in his life to raise a kid was just Andy's old fears and judgments biting him on the ass. Salt would build that man up until he knew no one could be the parent Ty needed but him.

He parked in the apartment building lot. It was almost dark. Salt had worked half the day before making the drive to the city. Carlos, cool boss that he was, had told Salt to take his time. That probably meant a few days at most, but Salt appreciated it.

Andy's apartment was on the fifth floor. Salt took the stairs—elevators made him borderline panicky. Someone had told him that there'd never been a case of an elevator cable crashing and sending people to their deaths, but he still hated the damned contraptions.

Five flights of stairs left him a little winded, but not too badly. He was in pretty good shape. Salt waited until his breathing was steady, then he lifted his hat up long enough to run a hand over his hair. Assured by the gesture, he settled the felt hat back in place and started looking for Andy's apartment.

He was nervous, a little concerned that Andy might not want him there in person. Then again, Salt believed the surest way to show Andy that he wasn't going to run off because of a kid was to make his presence known. Talking and texting was fine, but you couldn't see a person's expression and sometimes nothing was as reassuring as a hug.

Salt made sure his shirt was tucked in good then he knocked on the door. A few seconds later, he heard movement from inside the apartment. Then an exclamation. "Salt!" The door flew open and Salt was grabbed up into the arms of the man who meant the world to him. "You're here!"

"Yeah," Salt squeaked out as he was hugged tightly. Andy was definitely happy to see him, judging by the kisses landing all over Salt's face. Salt cupped Andy's chin and held him still for a deep, joyous kiss.

"Wow." Andy looked dazed as he blinked rapidly. "That was... I think you just made me fall in love with you all over again."

Oh, that was well beyond sweet. Salt had to fight not to blush. "Was worried about you. Carlos told me I can have a few days. If you want me here..."

Andy pulled back and gawped at him. "You have to ask that?"

Salt nodded. "Yeah, kinda, since we'd talked about me maybe having to stay a secret."

Andy's eyes went huge and he cursed softly. "Damn. Damn. I forgot, with everything going on. My lawyer's gay and he said a stable relationship would help not hinder my case. Gay or not. He thinks we can get a trial before a judge who'll be fair and not homophobic."

"You just now thought to tell me?" Salt wasn't sure if he should be offended or not. Probably not, he decided. Andy had a lot on his mind.

"He called me back last night and told me, once he'd done some checking on the judges here." Andy took his hand. "I should have called you then, but I crashed. Didn't think I'd be able to sleep, so I sat at the table and the next thing I knew, it was morning and there were cops banging on my door wanting to know about Ty showing up here. Let's sit down. I've been pacing, waiting to hear from them or Stratton, telling me they've got Ty and he's safe. I just want him to be safe."

Salt settled on the couch beside Andy, then he pulled Andy to him, almost across him for a hug they both needed. "You know I want to be there for you, and Ty. He might hate my guts, but I won't let him run me off."

"He won't hate you," Andy said assuredly. "He might hate me, but he won't hold that against you. Ty's a good kid, he's just understandably angry at me and Brandt." Andy twisted around to lie with his head in Salt's lap. "All Brandt wants is Ty's shares. I'll give him mine, same thing. That'll give Brandt a huge amount of the control, but..." Andy shrugged awkwardly. "Then I'll quit and he'll run the company into the ground."

"What about making it a legacy for Ty?" Salt asked as he stroked Andy's hair. "I thought Destry wanted that for him."

"He wanted Ty to be loved and cared for," Andy explained. "He will be, with us. Besides, I have Destry's business plans for other projects. The organic feed isn't all he wanted to start. He just ran out of time." Andy gave him a quirky grin. "We'll have to talk to Ty about it first, of course. I'm not making any decisions like that without his input. I learnt my lesson."

Salt used his free hand to take off his hat and toss it onto the coffee table. "You think you'll hear something today?"

"I'm hoping, but I didn't really have a great description of the kid Ty was with. I saw him, but I was so focused on Ty." Andy closed his eyes. "I keep trying to picture the guy, but I just get a generic image of a teenage boy. I don't even know if he had acne or not." Andy opened one eye. "Or if he was a boy. I just assumed."

"Maybe it was enough. Did that PI of yours ever access those records?"

"I don't know," Andy mumbled as he closed his eye. "I'm so tired. I shouldn't be. It's such a relief to have you here with me."

"I'm glad." Salt gently nudged Andy's shoulder. "Why don't we take a nap? I'm worn thin, too."

He let Andy help him up then they made their way to the bedroom. "This is a nice place. Bright colours and paintings on the walls. Looks like it was professionally decorated."

"Des was an ace at decorating. Most of what's done here is from him. Luckily, I can bring it with me if I move."

Salt stopped beside the bedroom door and looked at Andy. "Where would you move?" They hadn't really talked about that. "We've discussed us both being there for Ty, but we haven't discussed how that's gonna happen." Salt laughed and shook his head. "Man, we got to nail everything down."

"We do," Andy agreed, looking amused. "I guess I was thinking you and I would live together, and Ty with us, if it all works out."

Salt cocked and eyebrow at his lover. "Is that a roundabout way of asking me to move in?"

Andy glanced past him and licked his lips. "Well, see, I was thinking small-town life would probably be better for Ty."

Salt was almost dizzy with relief. "You want to move to Ashville?"

"If you'll have us." Andy sighed and focused on him. "If it all works out. We might be wasting our time on planning."

Salt didn't think so. "Damn right I'd welcome you both, and it's better to be prepared."

The smile lit up Andy's entire face. "Yeah, it is." He moved close to Salt, brushing their chests together. "I'm not so tired anymore."

Salt's cock perked up at that. "Yeah, me neither."

They grinned and Salt nudged Andy into the bedroom.

"Lock the door," Andy told him. "I've been leaving the front door unlocked, in case Ty shows up again."

"Sounds like a plan." Salt locked the door then put on what he hoped was a predatory smile. "Now why don't you get naked and let me ride you?"

Andy sucked in a sharp breath. "You, too. The naked part. All of it."

A babbling Andy was a very sexy man. Salt reached for his hat then remembered he'd left it in the living room. He backed up to the bed, sitting on the midnight-blue comforter. The bed itself was of the four-poster variety, made of dark red wood. Salt began tugging off his boots and Andy came right over.

"Allow me." Even dressed, Andy's ass looked divine when he turned his back to Salt and straddled his right leg. Salt's cock was fully erect and ready for Andy's touch. *Maybe too ready*, Salt mused. He glanced around the room rather than staring at Andy's butt. The walls were painted a light beige tone and the rest of the furniture matched the bed. On the wall closest to him hung a picture of a laughing Andy beside a man who was also laughing while holding a baby.

He didn't need to ask who the man and baby were. Salt knew. Destry resembled Andy a little, but he wouldn't have pegged them for brothers right off the bat.

"Other leg."

Salt put his right leg down and raised his left. Andy held it between his knees as he pulled on Salt's boot. "I have a boot jack," Andy said, grunting between every other word. "I just like doing this for you."

"I like you doing it for me, too." Salt was touched. No one else had ever been willing to do things like that for him.

Andy stripped off his boot and sock then patted his foot. "Now we can get naked."

Salt pointed at him. "You stay dressed. Just pull your pants and briefs down."

"Kinky," Andy teased. "I like it." He began unfastening his belt.

"Me too." Salt stood and quickly removed his clothes. Andy had his cock out and was stroking it in no time flat. "Want that in me."

"Come and get it." Andy shot past him and landed on his back on the bed. "Come on and ride me."

"Lube?" Salt wasn't fixing to take that monster cock without some slick and a finger or two.

"Under here." Andy dug under a pillow. "I was jerking off, thinking about you the night before last."

"This'll be better." Salt opened the lube and coated his fingers. "I'll do me, you do you."

"Deal." Andy caught the lube Salt tossed to him. "Turn around and let me watch."

Salt did as Andy asked, then reached behind him. He pulled one ass cheek back and used his other hand to tease along his crack.

"You're so fucking sexy," Andy rasped.

Salt hoped so. He didn't see it, but he sure hoped Andy did. He must have, Salt reasoned. Andy wouldn't lie to him.

"Bend over a little," Andy said.

Salt bent then touched his ass hole. "Yeah." *Damn, that feels good.* He teased the ring for a minute then pushed two fingers in, hard and fast. "Oh, hell."

"Fuck," Andy muttered. "So hot."

Andy was the hot one, with that deep, velvety voice. Salt moved his fingers around, opening himself up for his lover. He didn't do it for long, because his need was too great. He stopped fingering himself. "I'm ready."

"Come on up here then." Andy was patting his belly when Salt turned around. He held his cock pointing straight up, waving that big thing around. "Come and get it."

Salt almost laughed at that. "I sure as hell will."

He got up on the bed and straddled Andy's hips. "I got this." Reaching behind him, he kept his gaze locked with Andy's. He fisted Andy's thick shaft and pressed the tip to his hole. "You know I'm always gonna be here for you. You got me, heart and soul."

Andy's eyes looked a little misty as he replied. "Same goes, Salt. I want you in every way, so much."

"We'll start here." Salt sank down, that fat cock breaching him. It almost felt like being split open in the most pleasurable of ways. Andy's shaft stretched him to his limits and when Salt leant forward and rocked, it caused the most delicious contact between Andy's dick and Salt's prostate.

As good as it felt, Salt didn't sit still. He began a hard, rough ride, grinding down and shooting up, taking Andy into him over and over again. Andy reached up and pinched Salt's nipple and Salt moaned, closing his eyes. His dick was then encased in a firm, slick grip that shattered any lingering control he'd had.

Salt went after his climax like it was a gold trophy. He pressed his hands to Andy's thighs behind him and gyrated his hips, clenching his ass cheeks every time he came up.

"Come on, baby, give it up for me," he heard Andy demand.

Then Andy pressed against Salt's slit, a thumb or finger, he didn't know which. "Again!"

Andy worked his slit and Salt rode harder. Stars shot in gold and white streaks behind his closed lids as his orgasm slammed into him. He drove down and arched as he shot his load, Andy milking him with a demanding grip.

After he could breathe again, Salt yelped when he was flipped over. Andy pulled out of his ass. "On your belly. I've got to pound that ass."

Salt rolled over and got his knees up under him. He braced his head on his forearms. Andy didn't wait for more than that. He grabbed Salt by the hip and shoulder, then filled him in a quick thrust. Andy cursed and began hammering away at his ass. There was no finesse to it, the man was lost in his body's needs.

He dropped down over Salt and bit him on the shoulder before sucking the sting away. And he rumbled as he rammed his hips against Salt's ass. Hot spunk jetted into him. Salt felt every single shot. In his mind, it marked him inside as Andy's. He knew he was Andy's, and the man was his, but feeling Andy come inside him was never going to grow old.

Though the tickling as the cum seeped back out of him could stop. Salt remembered exactly how Andy had solved that problem last time.

As if reading his mind, Andy whispered, "Can't wait to lick you clean."

Salt shivered. "Stay inside of me a little longer?"

"As long as you want me to." Andy wrapped his arms around Salt and pulled him onto his side.

Chapter Sixteen

Another week passed and Andy was beginning to lose hope. Ty hadn't shown up, nor had he been found. The pre-paid cell phone number Ty had given to Andy always went right to voice mail. Giving the number to the cops had been a mistake, but one his attorney had told him he had to make. Andy hoped Ty would forgive him for it. The cops had said the phone was untraceable unless they could keep get Ty on the line and keep him there for a while. Even then, that was an expense the department wasn't likely to spend on a runaway who, they now believed, was safe and merely acting out.

Brandt was still a fucking asshole, and Salt had had to return to his job. Andy felt like his entire life was on hold. In a way, it was, but there was nothing he could do about it.

His attorney had everything ready to go if it came down to a court hearing. Brandt was nagging the shit out of him, trying to make him go out on sales calls, but Andy wasn't leaving until everything with Ty was settled. The company could fold if it came down to him having to go elsewhere.

As it was, Andy was making calls, literal ones, and there were some sales coming in. Nothing to rave about, but at least there were some.

He paced across the living room. Calling the cops in charge of Ty's case wouldn't do any good. He'd spoken to them for just that reason earlier in the morning. It pissed him off that Headly, the cop assigned to the case, always sounded like he was annoyed at Andy wanting to know about Ty.

A loud knock on the door sent a sense of foreboding over him. It just sounded like an angry knock. When he looked through the peephole, he knew why. Brandt stood on the other side of the door, glaring at him. Well, the peephole, but Andy knew who that anger was for.

He opened the door, glad that Brandt hadn't just barged in. Andy had barely spoken two sentences to Brandt since the ugly scene at Brandt's house. Everything Andy knew about Ty's disappearance had come from the cops or Ty.

He told himself to be patient and stay calm, not to let Brandt get to him. The little pep talk didn't brainwash him into believing things would go smoothly.

Andy opened the door. He stepped into the space between the door and the frame, not allowing Brandt inside. "What do you want?"

Brandt looked around the hallway. "Let me in."

"I don't think so. Maybe the threat of an audience will help you to be civil." It seemed like a brilliant plan to Andy.

Brandt looked fit to be tied, his face and neck flushing with visual proof of his ire. "You need to get back to work."

"I *am* working," Andy pointed out. "I made three sales this week already, none of them small." Yet none were spectacular, but Brandt was lucky Andy had done that much.

"You need to get on the road and make sales calls in person."

Andy smiled slightly. "No, I don't. I'm not leaving until I know Ty is safe."

"He was safe!" Brandt glanced around nervously, then said quieter, "He was safe with me. I never hit him."

"You never loved him, either." Andy stood up a little straighter. "All he was to you was a way to hurt me and to control the majority of the company's stock. He heard you say so."

Brandt shook with, Andy suspected, a raw fury that had always been inside him. "So what? He had a roof over his head, and food, clothes, school. He didn't need anything else. He could be an outsider in his own home just like I was."

Andy barely kept from decking Brandt right then. "You made yourself that outsider. Nothing me or Brandt could say or do ever made you love us. You were born hateful, and you're gonna die hateful, but that hate is never going to touch me or Ty again."

"You think you have a chance at custody?" Brandt sneered.

Andy grinned. "If Ty wants to live with me, yeah. Courts won't look too kindly on the head games you played with him. And by the way, you want the company? Once I have Ty, you can have my shares. I'm done partnering with you. If Ty wants to sell his, you can make him a fair offer, but the choice to sell will be his."

Brandt narrowed his eyes at Andy. "I don't believe you."

Andy shrugged. "Not my problem." Then he took a step back and slammed the door on Brandt. There was nothing else to discuss.

Brandt knocked again, but Andy ignored him. He set the lock, figuring it would be okay for this one time. Then he went and called his lawyer. Stratton would know what to do with the news of this visit.

Thirty minutes later, there was another knock on Andy's door. He rolled his eyes. At least Brandt wasn't trying to pound the door down. Andy undid the lock then opened the door without checking the peephole. "Look—" He stopped cold when he saw Ty standing outside. "Ty." Andy swallowed against the sudden tightness in his throat.

"I don't want to get my friend in trouble," Ty mumbled. "So I guess I gotta turn myself in."

"You're not a criminal," Andy said as he reached for Ty, only to pull his hand back.

"Cops have been looking for me. I feel like a criminal." Ty sniffled and turned red-rimmed eyes up to Andy. "I'm tired of hiding, and I... I wanted to see Dad's room. Can—Did you change it?"

"No, didn't change yours, either." Andy stepped back. "Come in. You are always welcome here. I've kept the door unlocked since your last visit, except for the past half hour or so. Brandt stopped by."

Ty took a step back. "He's not here?"

"No, I sent him on his way. Please, Ty," Andy pleaded softly. "Please, come in. Come home."

Ty sobbed and darted into the apartment, bumping Andy as he passed. Andy didn't complain. He shut and locked the door, then watched Ty go into his dad's room.

Andy rubbed his temples, trying to keep from doing a little crying himself. Things were so fucked up between him and Ty, and they used to be so close. "We'll have that again." Andy would make sure of it.

But he had to do everything the right way, starting off with what was legal. Andy took out his cell phone again and called Stratton.

"Andy? What's happened? Did your brother come back?"

Andy looked at Destry's closed door. "No, but Ty did. I think he wants to come home. To me."

Stratton's sigh sounded like a relieved one. "Good. Good, I was worried about him. Usually your PI can track down anyone. When she couldn't find Ty after his visit, I was concerned. It's fantastic that he's safe." Stratton cleared his throat. "Now, has he said specifically that he wants to live with you? Would he be willing to talk to me? Have you called the police yet?"

Andy's head reeled from all the questions. "Uh. I'm not sure, and I don't know, and no."

Stratton said something unintelligible to someone, maybe a secretary for all Andy knew. Then he came back on the phone. "Okay. I need you to talk to him, see if he'll talk to me, consent to me recording the conversation. Ask him point-blank if he wants to remain with you. And I'll handle the cops."

"Okay, I can do that." Andy felt better knowing what to do, the steps to take.

"I'm also going to have Brandt served with a restraining order. You said he appeared threatening and you were scared to let him into your home."

Andy hadn't been scared. "I just wanted to avoid a fight."

"Which you think would have happened, had Brandt been allowed inside — a physical fight. And he did attack you first once before."

"But he didn't actually hit me," Andy reiterated. "I ducked."

"That's beside the point. It will also help should there be a custody case."

Andy sighed and pinched the bridge of his nose. "Okay then. I trust you to do what's best."

"Thank you. I'll be in touch in a few hours."

Andy disconnected the call and tucked his phone in his pocket. Then he took it back out and sent Salt a quick text letting him know things were probably about to come to a head. He sent a second one telling him Ty was there, and he was about to go speak with him.

That done, he returned the phone to his shirt pocket and started for the hallway. Before he reached Destry's bedroom door, he could hear the muffled sobs coming from the room.

"Shit. *Shit.*" Guilt slammed into him. He tapped at the door. "Ty? Ty, can I come in, please?"

Whatever Ty's garbled reply meant, Andy chose to believe it was a 'yes'. He opened the door and his heart broke at the sight that greeted him. Ty was curled up on the bed, hugging one of Destry's pillows as he cried.

"Oh, God, honey, I'm so sorry." Andy rushed to the bed. "Ty, please. I'm sorry."

Ty's blue eyes were puffy, his face red. He looked so young and scared that Andy couldn't stand it.

"Please, Ty. I swear I'll never do anything so stupid again. I can't take back what's happened, what I did, but I will never let you feel like you aren't loved, like you don't have a home."

"I lost everything," Ty whispered. "I don't know if I can forgive you."

Andy sat down on the floor beside the bed. He folded his hands together and stared at them. "I understand. You don't have to forgive me, just...just let me take care of you. Me and Salt, he's my partner. You'll like him, and he hasn't done you wrong."

"P-partner?" Ty got out as he rubbed his nose on his shirt sleeve. "Is he here?"

Andy shook his head as the first tear escaped. "Nah. He's a cowboy on a ranch outside of Ashville. A real calm guy. He'd never have let someone get away with taking someone he loved. He's...he's pretty awesome, Ty. He wants to meet you."

When Ty didn't speak, Andy looked at him. It must have been what Ty was waiting for.

"I don't know. I just want to come home, but I don't know where that is anymore."

Andy hoped he didn't screw up and say the wrong thing. He was aching to have his nephew back in his life. "If you'll let me, and Salt, we'll show you where home is. What home is. I don't believe it's a place. I believe it's where your heart feels safest and you know you're loved."

Ty started sobbing quietly again, and Andy had to risk being rejected. If Ty needed him, then he was going to be there. Andy leaned over and opened up his arms. Ty hesitated, then he slid off the bed and curled into Andy's embrace. With Ty being nearly his height, it should have been awkward, but all Andy could think was how perfect it felt.

There were questions that Stratton needed answers to, but for that moment in time, nothing else was as important as holding Ty.

Eventually, the crying ceased and Ty went slack against him as sleep carried the boy away. Andy stood, bringing Ty up with him. He got Ty onto the bed and tried to cover him up, then he left the room.

He had messages from Salt. Andy didn't even read them, instead calling Salt. He needed to hear Salt's voice. Afterwards, he'd do what needed to be done.

* * * *

The next morning, Andy woke up feeling as if he'd been out partying the night before. He hadn't. There'd been police at his house and Brandt throwing a hissy fit when he'd been served with a restraining order. Child services had been called when Ty refused to go back to Brandt's house, and now the ball was in a completely different court.

Andy had felt like the biggest fraud when Ty had been taken by the state workers. Ty should have been there with him, but due to Brandt's attempt to retain custody, and Ty's vow to run away again if he were returned to Brandt, there was going to be an investigation by Child and Family Services to determine what—and who—was best for Ty.

All Andy could do was hope Ty believed him when he told the boy he didn't want him to leave. That Child and Family Services weren't giving him a choice. The social worker had told Ty as much, too, but still. It was too similar to the way Andy had let him go before.

Andy's cell rang with the ring tone he'd assigned Brandt. Apparently the ass didn't understand what being served a restraining order meant. Curious, Andy answered the phone. "You are in violation of a court order."

"This is Mary," his sister in law said. "Not Brandt."

Andy wasn't too sure what the rules were regarding that. He was sure Brandt had put her up to it.

"Okay, and what do you want?"

"The shares. You promised you'd give them up."

He should have known. "You don't get them and Ty, too."

"We don't want Ty. *I* don't want Ty. Brandt can deal with letting his weapon against you slip away. I don't want to raise someone else's kid."

"Why, Mary, you're all heart."

Mary huffed. "Oh, up yours! You don't know what it's like!"

He did, actually. He'd helped raise Ty up until he'd stupidly let Brandt and Mary manipulate him. Arguing that wasn't going to get him anywhere. "I tell you what. You call my lawyer, and ask him to draft papers saying Brandt gives up all claims to Ty. Do what he says about that, and once it's all filed with the court or Child and Family Services, I'll sign over my shares."

"What's the number?" she asked unhesitatingly.

Andy gave it to her then hung up. Hopefully he would never have to speak to her or Brandt again. He dialled Stratton's number and left him a voicemail explaining what had just happened with Mary.

Then Andy called Salt, and after a short conversation, Salt told him he was on his way to Andy's place.

Andy needed him, so much. He didn't protest.

* * * *

It seemed as if everything was going to get worked out, Salt decided as he drove to the city. He just hoped to hell it all worked out in Andy's favour. It sure sounded like Ty was going to end up with Andy. Eventually.

Salt would wait. He'd promised to, and if necessary, he could live in the city, in an apartment. It wasn't something he'd ever wanted, but he did want Andy. For him, Salt would give up everything.

The drive passed quickly, considering how bad he wanted to hold Andy. Salt was a little nervous, because he knew there was a chance he was going to be checked out by the agency caring for Ty. There was nothing bad on his record, no criminal arrests or anything like that, but it was still creepy.

He parked the truck and unbuckled. The sun was peeking out between clouds when he got out. Salt strode across the parking lot, a duffel bag in hand. He was glad it was Saturday. He was going to owe Rocky a bunch of favours for trading days off with him again.

Her maybe-girlfriend Jen was going to serve him cold coffee at the diner.

Salt jogged up the stairs and grinned when he reached the fifth floor with little effort. When he knocked on Andy's door, it didn't take but two seconds for the door to be opened and Andy to be in his arms.

"Thank you for coming," Andy said against his cheek.

"Always. Anytime you need me." Salt took a deep breath then canted his head back to look into Andy's eyes. "I can stay, permanently, if you want."

Andy's expression was priceless as the man sputtered. "But—your job!"

Salt shrugged and hoped his expression hid the sadness he felt at possibly quitting. "It's just a job. A good one, yeah, but I won't be doing it forever, and I want forever, with you. I want to be a part of your and Ty's family, so if that means quitting, then I will quit."

"Don't go jumping off cliffs without a parachute," Andy advised. "Let's see what Stratton and the child agency says. I don't want you to quit. One of us will need to have a job." Andy smiled crookedly. "It'd look bad if we were both unemployed."

"You're going to give him the shares?" Salt didn't want Brandt to have anything, but he understood Andy's reasoning.

"If he signs away any rights to Ty, yeah. And I'll quit." Andy drooped a little, his shoulders rounding. "I haven't gotten to talk to Ty about that yet. I need to before I do anything for sure."

"You'll do that." Salt moved them into the apartment and kicked the door shut with his heel. "Any idea when you can see him?"

Andy gripped his hand. "No. I haven't heard anything yet this morning. Stratton told me to be patient, but it's so hard."

"He'll be allowed to come back to you." Salt didn't doubt it.

"I hope so. I just want him happy, and I want you." Andy looked at him so tenderly it made Salt's heart flutter.

"You got me, I told you that. And you can quit, I'll stay on at the ranch. I can come down on the days I get off. Carlos will give me a five-day work week. He told me so." Salt generally worked six days a week, because he wasn't an idle man. That, and there was always something that needed doing on a ranch the size of the Mossy G.

"I need to thank your bosses for being so great about this." Andy didn't stop at the couch. He kept walking until they reached his bedroom. "Need to thank you, too. We started out as a little fun, and now — you didn't bargain for this."

"But I'll gladly take it," Salt asserted. "I will most certainly, gladly, take it."

Andy caressed his cheek. "It's going to be hard, and invasive, with Child and Family Services sticking their noses in our business. Ty might not want to move from this apartment. It was his home for a long time."

Salt knew that was a real possibility. "That's okay. He needs to be comfortable, needs to feel secure. As for hard, I'm a cowboy. We're made of hard, sugar. I don't have any business for that place to be up in, but they can snoop around. Whatever it takes to make you happy."

"You make me happy." Andy moved closer and kissed him, a bare touch of lips that made Salt yearn for more. "You. Come make love with me. I need you."

"As much as I need you." Salt followed Andy into the bedroom and locked the door.

Chapter Seventeen

Nothing worthwhile ever came easy, Salt reminded himself as a net full of butterflies was unleashed in his stomach. He'd had a background check run on him and been vetted by all kinds of state people just so this moment could happen. And now he was so nervous he thought he might throw up.

Andy took Salt's hand and gave it a light squeeze. "It's gonna be fine. Ty's a good kid. He'll love you, given a little time."

Despite Andy's assurances, Salt had his doubts. After all, Ty might see him as competition for Andy's attention. He might resent Salt, and what did he have to offer a kid, anyway?

"Breathe," Andy ordered in a soft voice. "Stop thinking about everything that could go wrong, and think about the step we're taking today."

Salt cleared his throat, trying to clear away the nerves at the same time. He shuffled his feet and ran his free hand down the buttons of his shirt.

Andy caught that hand, too, and held it as Salt glanced at him. "Salt. Trust me. You've been through the wringer for this. The child services people think it's time, and so does Ty. You need to trust yourself, and Ty. He really wants to meet you."

"I just don't know what I've got to offer the kid," Salt murmured, afraid, so afraid of letting Ty and Andy down. Himself, too, because damn, but he wanted the family that was within his grasp. "I'm just an old cowboy—"

Andy snorted and let go of his hands. "Oh, now don't start that crap up. You're more than just a cowboy, and you aren't old. Seasoned, a bit, but that just makes you wiser than the rest of us. Ty is going to be following you around wanting to *be* you. What boy doesn't want to be a cowboy?"

"Lots of boys," Salt retorted, thinking of a dozen scenarios where this first meeting went to hell. "Otherwise we'd have too many cowboys running around."

Andy pursed his lips and looked up at the ceiling. Salt knew he was trying to come up with another argument, or more likely, another way to set Salt at ease. That just wasn't going to happen until Ty showed up with the case worker and Salt got a better idea of whether the kid was going to hate him or not.

"He's a good kid," Andy finally reiterated. "He wants to meet you, and he wants to come home."

"To the apartment," Salt couldn't help but point out. God, but he didn't want to live in the city. He would, if Ty and Andy were going to stay there. And if Ty didn't hate him. He would hate the city, and feel as lost as a kitten in a wolf pack, but he'd deal with it.

"To me," Andy said, taking Salt's hand again. "And you. He wants a family, and we're it for him now that Brandt isn't allowed around him."

Which was a great thing, in Salt's opinion. Harsh, maybe, but Brandt had refused to do anything the children's services agency had asked him to do in order to see Ty. Plus, Ty wanted nothing to do with the ass.

Salt twitched a little when the doorknob turned, then his heart did a slow, heavy thud as the door was opened. A solemn young man stepped into the widening space. Ty looked so much like Andy it made Salt's eyes tear up.

Ty turned big, dark eyes on him, and hesitated with the door halfway open. His lips moved, like he wanted to say something but couldn't get the words out. Dressed in a pair of new jeans, cowboy boots, a shirt with pearl snaps up the front and a felt cowboy hat, the kid gulped then came into the room. The caseworker, Mrs Jeanine, followed him and shut the door.

Andy stepped forward and held out a hand. "Mrs Jeanine." Salt did the same, finding a smile that he was sure showed his nervousness. Mrs Jeanine returned his smile and gave him a sympathetic look. *Relax*, she mouthed at him. Salt nodded jerkily, then she let go of his hand and Ty was right there, sliding between him and Mrs Jeanine.

The boy was tall, probably five-ten or so. Maybe that wasn't tall for his age, Salt didn't know, but he liked the way Ty held himself, shoulders up and back straight.

"Salt Johnson," he said as he held his hand out to Ty.

Ty licked his lips and when he spoke, his voice cracked in that way only puberty could cause. "Ty Calder."

"Good grip you got there." Salt couldn't keep back a grin. Ty's palm was every bit as sweaty as his own.

"My mama always said you could tell what kind of man you're dealing with by his grip. A confident man has a strong grip, but not so's he's trying to prove his strength."

Ty released Salt's hand. "My dad said the same thing, just about. He believed a handshake meant something. He told me an honourable man could be trusted to keep his word, if he shook hands on it."

Salt nodded. "Yup. That's the way it should be." Then he didn't know what to say, and there was an awkward moment as he and Ty shuffled their feet.

Mrs Jeanine put a hand on Ty's shoulder and stepped up beside him. "Well, Mr Johnson, Ty has certainly been looking forward to this meeting. I have, too, because I am very impressed with your willingness to do what we've requested of you. And taking the parenting classes, that was..." She shook her head. "Well, I just wish more people cared about kids the way you do. Too many aren't willing to do anything that inconveniences them, yet you drove in every week for the classes. I am impressed, that's for sure."

Salt was blushing so fiercely he thought he might catch on fire. He'd taken parenting classes, that was true. One set the agency was requiring, and another because he wanted to be as good at helping Andy with Ty as he possibly could be. It seemed to him, despite all the talking in those lessons, that being a parent was a mixture of common sense and a lot of love. There were other things, of course, but he thought those two were the most important.

"You're really red," Ty told him. "I think you embarrassed him, Mrs Jeanine."

Salt grunted, and Andy chuckled before he spoke. "Salt is a modest man, sure enough."

"He is, indeed," Mrs Jeanine agreed. "That's a good quality in a man."

"Yes, it is. I think—"

"I'm standing right here," Salt pointed out, cutting Andy off. Andy winked at him.

Ty cocked his head to one side and met Salt's gaze. "They tend to do that, talk around a person. Like we either aren't supposed to point out how rude that is, or we're not smart enough to realise they're talking about us right in front of us."

"Hey!" Andy yelped. "That wasn't what we were doing!"

Mrs Jeanine tutted and shook her head. "I think Ty's right, about us talking around Mr Johnson and him." She turned her attention to Ty. "But you're wrong about us not thinking you're smart. Maybe we don't expect to get called on being rude, though."

Ty widened his eyes, and Salt was suddenly sure the kid was working Mrs Jeanine. "Sorry, ma'am."

She huffed out a laugh and patted Ty's shoulder. "You know you have nothing to apologise for. Now you're just making sure I feel guilty."

Ty opened his mouth then shut it. He looked Salt straight in the eyes. "Dad also told me to be direct when there was something I wanted."

Salt nodded. "Yeah, I'd say that's best." He tried not to fidget as Ty studied him for a long moment.

Then Ty inhaled, and exhaled on a question. "Do you really want me? Or are you just doing this all for Uncle Andy? I don't want to be in the way, or...or unwanted."

Salt had never been more glad for the counselling and parenting classes as he was then. He'd been told to expect something similar because Ty would need to know he wasn't being thought of as a burden. Salt knew the kid wouldn't be. As much as he wanted to hug Ty, he was afraid that would be too much for the kid, so he needed words to offer Ty reassurance.

Salt gestured at the uncomfortable sofa in the visiting room. "Can we sit down and talk, get to know each other a little? I think that would help us both more than me just telling you that yes, I really do want to be a part of your life, and not all just for Andy, though I do love the man more and more each day."

Andy made a happy little sound and Mrs Jeanine went back to the door. "I'm just going to grab a drink, then I'll be right back, sitting at the table. Anyone else want anything?"

"No, ma'am," Ty said, along with Andy and Salt. Mrs Jeanine left the room, but didn't close the door all the way.

"Guess she can't close it," Andy muttered. "Supervised visit and all."

"It's okay." Salt offered Andy a smile before looking at Ty. "I'm real glad to finally get to meet you, Ty. You look so much like Andy and your daddy. I hope you'll be happy living with us."

Ty nibbled on his bottom lip as he stared at the ground. Salt slowly reached out and put a hand on Ty's back. "You want to have a seat?"

Instead of answering, Ty turned and headed for the couch. Salt sat on one end and Ty on the other, but they weren't leaning away from each other, which Salt considered a good thing.

"What would you like to ask me?" Salt began, wanting to give Ty free rein on the conversation. "Or is there something you'd like to tell me about yourself?"

Ty snorted and looked up at him then. "They made you see a therapist, didn't they?"

Salt had hated it, too. "Yeah, but they required a psych evaluation on Andy and me, too."

Ty scrunched up his nose. "Brandt refused, and I'm glad. I don't want to see him ever again." Then Ty turned a fierce look on Andy. "And he can't have the company. No way. Dad wanted it for me, and Brandt can't have my shares. I've been thinking about that. I trust *you* with my shares, not Brandt. Can we keep the company going even if he has some stock in it?"

Andy squatted then sat on the floor between them. "We can. We can do that, and hire someone else for sales, because I'm not going to be running all over the US anymore. I want to be home with you and Salt."

Ty plumb beamed at Andy, then he turned to Salt with a little less enthusiasm and a hint of reserve. "Do you even like kids? Did you want any?" Before Salt could answer, Ty's voice dipped lower and for once didn't crack. "You don't want to be my dad, right? I have a dad. Just because he died doesn't mean he's not still my dad."

Salt's heart was going to crumble under the boy's pain. Ty's chin quivered and his eyes grew teary. Salt wanted once again to hug him, but was afraid it'd freak Ty out. "I like kids just fine, Ty. I haven't been around many, but that don't mean I don't like them. Just never had much chance, working on ranches and such. As for wanting any?" Salt couldn't keep back the smile pulling at his lips. "I gotta say, you're a blessing I never thought to have in my life. I figured, when I first realised I was gay, that kids were out of the question."

"People adopt—" Ty began, but Salt was already shaking his head.

"That's true, but cowboys who are in the closet don't," Salt pointed out. "And I was in the closet, or else I'd have been out of a job most of my workin' life. Now, the Mossy Glenn? That's a ranch that you don't have to be in the closet to work at. For the first time in my life, I've found out what it's like to be free." Salt swallowed as he looked at Andy. "To love someone so much you can't imagine how you've lived so long without them."

Andy took his hand. "Ditto, Salt. You know I love you and want to spend the rest of my life with you."

Salt heard Mrs Jeanine come back in but she didn't speak and so he ignored her. She had her job to do, and he had a family to prove himself to. "I am plumb tickled to have a chance to know you, Ty. I know I'm not your daddy, but I hope I can be someone you come to trust and rely on. Someone you know loves you and will take care of you."

Ty sniffled and tipped his head down. "I'd like that."

"Then we'll make it happen," Salt promised, and he'd never meant anything more than he meant that vow he made then.

After that, talking seemed to come easier for him and Ty both. Salt wasn't surprised to find the boy bright and articulate. He knew, too, that Ty was going to have him wrapped around Ty's little finger, because the smile the kid gave him—that genuine, happy smile—was going to make it hard for Salt to ever be irritated when Ty did something wrong.

By the end of the visit, Salt was a lot less nervous about helping to raise Ty than he'd been over the past months.

"It's going to be okay," Andy promised, as if knowing Salt's concerns. "This is going to work out and we're all going to be happy. Well, Brandt won't, but that's his tough luck. He's a fool to give up such an amazing kid."

"Glad as hell he did," Salt growled. "He sure doesn't deserve Ty, or any pity."

"I don't pity him. I wish he wasn't a dick, though. I'd like to have a brother again." Andy swiped a hand down his face. "Don't think I can claim Brandt after all he's done. Maybe he'll sell his shares to me or Ty..."

Salt didn't say anything else as they walked to the truck. Whatever Brandt decided to do with the shares was out of his hands, and the company itself would be out from under Brandt's control.

"I'm glad you're not tossing the company," he said a few minutes later when they were on the road. "You put a lot into it."

"So did Destry." Andy sighed. "He'd be sad to see what had happened with Brandt and he'd probably beat my ass over letting Ty go live with Brandt, but we're going to make it all right."

"We are," Salt agreed, putting his hand on Andy's thigh. "We really are."

Epilogue

It wasn't nervousness making Salt's palms sweat. He was plumb excited. Finally, after months of counselling and relationship-building with him, Andy and Ty, they were really going to be a family.

After that first meeting with Ty, things had progressed a little faster, but it'd still seemed like he and Andy had jumped through every hoop in the world so that they could all be a family. Ty had opened up to him more and more with every visit, and Salt was amazed at what a bright, loving young man Ty was.

Giving, too. Ty hadn't thrown a hissy and insisted on living in the city. In fact, the kid loved visiting the Mossy G, and everyone at the ranch thought the sun rose and set over Ty. With a few years' experience, Ty'd be every bit the cowboy he wanted to be. With the company growing more successful every month, Ty might even be able to buy his own ranch by the time he finished college.

I'd never have thought I'd have this. Love, a family, a job that suits me down to a T. Man oh man, life don't get any better. Salt found himself thinking those very things over and over. But, life really *was* about to get even better.

Soon, very soon, Andy and Ty would be arriving, and staying at the ranch for good. It was going to be their home, and that was more perfect than anything else Salt could have imagined. He loved the Mossy G, and he loved Andy and Ty. He was grateful every day that he hadn't had to give up his job and go live in the city. Glad, too, that he didn't have to live in Ashville or somewhere off the Mossy G's land.

Carlos, Troy and Will had been great about it all. They'd allowed him the time off he'd needed to do what he'd had to so Ty could live with him and Andy. Then there'd been the big thing they'd done — offering them a home on the ranch.

Salt had been allowed to convert the unused bunkhouse into a home for him, Andy and Ty. It'd meant a small cut in his pay, but that was all right. It was less than renting a place. It was also theirs for as long as Salt worked there, and when he retired? He and Andy could still live there. Salt had been deeply moved by his bosses' generosity.

Then he'd been moved by the kindness of everyone he worked with. The other ranch hands had thrown in their support and helped him get the bunkhouse fixed up. Even Ramsey, who still got on Salt's nerves. The man had worked there for going on nine months, and Salt was just as suspicious of him today as he'd been at the get-go.

Well, there was nothing he could do about it. Instead he thought of the walls of the house he'd painted a fine, pale blue and the rugs Rocky had thrown down on the floor.

For the first time in ages, Salt had a *home*. He'd spent almost as much time working on it as he had working at his job. Between those two things, and the weekly trips to visit Andy and Ty, Salt was worn out.

But he was so damned happy he could burst from it.

Ty was a good kid, too. Not perfect. He had his evil spawn teen moments, but all in all, he was great. It'd taken him little time at all to warm up to Salt after that first visit. Salt had fallen for the kid in less time than that.

Salt thought they were all pretty solid now. Ty wanted to move, wanted them to be a family, and he wanted away from the city. Most of the things his daddy Destry had used to decorate that apartment with were now in the home Salt, and all of the cowhands, had helped prepare.

Salt could hardly wait to see the house with Andy and Ty actually living in it. On their previous visits, they'd stayed in either the big house or the bunkhouse with the other employees. But now they'd all have a home.

"What time are they coming?" Rocky asked.

Salt nailed the tin down then hung the hammer on his tool belt. "Couple more hours. Andy said he and Ty were going to take the long way, see a few sights. Don't know what sights, but considering I have to work until five or six —"

Rocky flapped a hand at him. "Any chance they told you that just so they could surprise you?"

Salt went still then he turned slowly on the rooftop, not wanting to go ass over tea kettle off the damn barn. Sure enough, there was Andy's truck pulling up to the converted bunkhouse.

"Rocky, will you —"

"Go on," Rocky snorted. "Jen is gonna have your balls."

Salt glanced at her. "What'd she want 'em for?" He grinned as she laughed, then he made his way to the edge of the roof where the ladder was.

He climbed down carefully, and when he reached the bottom rung, Andy and Ty were there waiting for him.

Salt barely got turned around before he was being hugged by his two favourite guys. "Welcome home."

"Home isn't a place, Salt," Ty said, smiling so happily at him that it was almost painful to see. "It's where your heart feels safe, where you know you're loved."

Salt nodded, looking into Andy's eyes. "Yeah. Like I said, welcome home."

About the Author

A native Texan, Bailey spends her days spinning stories around in her head, which has contributed to more than one incident of tripping over her own feet. Evenings are reserved for pounding away at the keyboard, as are early morning hours. Sleep? Doesn't happen much. Writing is too much fun, and there are too many characters bouncing about, tapping on Bailey's brain demanding to be let out.

Caffeine and chocolate are permanent fixtures in Bailey's office and are never far from hand at any given time. Removing either of those necessities from Bailey's presence can result in what is know as A Very, Very Scary Bailey and is not advised under any circumstances.

Bailey Bradford loves to hear from readers. You can find her contact information, website details and author profile page at http://www.totallybound.com.

Totally Bound Publishing